Why Ghosts Are Afraid of the Living

By

JGC O'Connell

MAPLE
PUBLISHERS

Why Ghosts Are Afraid of the Living

Author: JGC O'Connell

Copyright © 2024 JGC O'Connell

The right of JGC O'Connell to be identified as author of this work has been asserted by the author in accordance with section 77 and 78 of the Copyright, Designs and Patents Act 1988.

First Published in 2024

ISBN 978-1-83538-292-9 (Paperback)
       978-1-83538-293-6 (E-Book)

Book Cover Design and Book Layout by:
      White Magic Studios
      www.whitemagicstudios.co.uk

Published by:
      Maple Publishers
      Fairbourne Drive, Atterbury,
      Milton Keynes,
      MK10 9RG, UK
      www.maplepublishers.com

A CIP catalogue record for this title is available from the British Library.

DEDICATION

To My great friend Marion Scott

11 April 1962 – 10th November 2023

Such a beautiful soul, Jx

The first book of "Why"

Why Ghosts are afraid of the Living

**People are scary to ghosts, just as ghosts
can be to people.**

*I was told this long ago by Arthur and I know
that it is so in my case. People worry and scare
me - so I try to avoid them where possible.
However, this can be hard to do sometimes,
especially when they seek you out.*

Chapter 1

On Passing Over

When you pass, a new world opens up. It is an amazingly colourful world, almost too bright, to start with. That is until you adjust your senses, tweak the dimmer switch. I say 'senses' because you don't have eyes to see, though you do still see. All of your senses are more alive and you have many more senses to boot. They are just not the same senses you have been used to whilst being confined in a body. What I mean, is that you sense everything at once, more intensely than you ever have before, but you don't have the same senses as before. Does this sound confusing? I will attempt to channel the immensity of the experience to "J O", so that he may be better able to communicate this.

There is the going towards the light which appears as if through a long-darkened tunnel. Similar to the view through a telescope. And yes, your life, achievements and failures flash through your thoughts. The soul (if I can call this energy that is ME, that), does appear to float above what was your physical body too and you look back down at your dead self. But it is so much more than that. A release from the chastity of physical containment. The instant communication with all that surrounds you. It can be overwhelming, but also beautiful. At the end of the tunnel - if there is a tunnel, you suddenly emerge as if from a womb, and you are greeted by those who have known you, and others, who you feel you know already. You are judged - not harshly - just weighed against your life's achievements (for want of a better word, as failures are successes too). And the burden of your life is greedily shared amongst the surrounding energies of which you are part. We are all one. A massive weight lifts from your shoulders. You should know that the things which worry the living on a daily basis, and lead people to self-harm, mentally as well as physically, are mainly pointless. You become one with the other souls which make up the universe. Whatever you did in life, you instantly know, was not wrong. It is as if you have a massive laugh at yourself. Laughter in the release of the confusion of the living, of being alive. A laughter which for a brief moment echoes around the universe. And then you are spoken to. You have many options - but within an instant billions of avenues are open to you, evaluated and you are told (and also, decide) your fate. I was told that it wasn't quite my time yet, I had to return. But I wasn't to return to my body. I was to become what some may interpret as 'a ghost'. I had to come back. Something had to be resolved. I was needed to try to solve an issue, I had a purpose, a mission. And within an instant, without further knowledge of my task, I appeared back at this semi-derelict abandoned house. The one in which I passed.

It was slightly confusing at first. After the euphoria of being born again - which is almost what death is. Even more so, because the house in which I passed over had become more desolate and decayed. Items were scattered all over, windows smashed, doors hanging on hinges, drawers opened, floorboards exposed and rotten. Dampness all around, with a multitude of smells. This didn't bother me though. I had been returned for a reason and that reason would become apparent in time. Until then I would endure anything that came my way. It took me a while to adjust - until I realised that several years must have gone by since my actual death. Had I been in that place at the end of the tunnel for these years - or had I moved forward in time? I could no longer look down and see my body - so I must have been buried, I assumed. There were insects, spiders and other life-forms dashing about like sprinklings of lights. Life is all over the place. As a 'ghost' you smile at them, and they give you a greeting, changing colours when you pass them by. Animals sense and respect Ghosts. And you no longer hold any fear, disgust, repulsion or animosity towards any of these living creatures. All life makes you smile now. All is so wondrous. All twinkles and all move on about their given path in their life-journey. Everything has a purpose.

It was shortly after this that I met Arthur. It was the smell of pipe smoke I noticed at first. I had been wandering the rooms, looking at old photos of past residents, reading some discarded letters which I blew across the floor to turn over. This is a new sense, and one of the many you achieve through death that doesn't exist in life. The ability to move objects without physical touch. So I turned these pages over. But for all intents and purposes they blew over as I did not need to use the hands I no longer had, but used the inner eye - so to speak - to get them to flip over. If I had been lazy enough I could have read the reverse of the letters without moving them at all. But being newly dead, I suppose that I was still exploring my abilities as it had only been for what I guess was a couple of days since my return.

Curiously, I wasn't shocked to find that I wasn't the only one here. I suppose that the house lent itself to what could be considered a haunted building because of its age and dilapidation. As I mentioned, the first thing I noticed was the strong waft of pipe tobacco. Though Arthur later explained that he couldn't, as a ghost, actually smoke a pipe. It was something which he held on to from his living state and sort of defined him. He came in through the veranda, double doors which led onto the back garden area. He was very casual in his initial greeting. After a raise of the eyebrows, said politely, "Good evening, madam." He then introduced himself and we got into a conversation. After all, it had been perhaps a couple of days - possibly three since I had communicated with another Soul and I was eager to converse. When I introduced myself and gave him my name he told me that he was aware of who I was. This piqued my curiosity further.

Chapter 2

On Energy, and Achievement

Arthur lit his pipe. Or rather went through the motions of lighting it as it never actually burnt but was more of a prop. But it was reassuring for him to puff away, as he had in life, and it was a comfort to him to waft around the place smelling of pipe tobacco. He pretended to wave away some of the non-existent smoke as if it irritated him and proceeded to explain, "We all have a reason for being, my girl!" As an aside, he stated, "Sorry if that sounds patronising but that is what you were in your last life that is what you appear at the moment and how you manifest your energy to me. As a young lady."

He chuckled gruffly and asked, "Who can tell the future? You may come back as a big strapping lad working with Shire Horses, like Young Andy Bateman, whom I used to know!" As an afterthought, he added, "...before he went off and was killed in the Great War, Tut tut!" He shook his head.

Let me explain and introduce Arthur. He was an elderly Presence - in the region of 60-65 years of age, short in stature, ever so slightly portly around the midriff. His face was as friendly as a typical grandfather figure would be. Head bald on top, but tufts of grey above each ear joined around the back of his head with a thick line of smooth, silver hair. He wore a tweed waistcoat, over a cotton shirt, with tweed trousers, and very firm leather shoes – which were almost boots. On his waistcoat, he had a silver pocket watch, tucked into one of the pockets, connected to a silver chain. This was his last persona, and because he hasn't yet fully passed over like me, he still manifests himself in the way he feels most comfortable. In his last life, he had been a General Practitioner - a local doctor in the village. His wife Irene, whom he sometimes called 'Reeney' - he remembers fondly. "She would've passed straight over and probably had a couple more lives since then," he later remarked. As, he felt, his two boys, Harold and Cecil, probably had gone on to greater lives too.

Arthur elaborated, "Cecil I believe stayed at home, but Harold went off to the 2nd Great War and was killed in the desert. I know, as I had been whipping around trying to help the living where I could, as a ghost can in limited ways. I was informed of his passing - like an astral telegraph - and, in an instant, was able to be with him to ease him across to the great beyond! Baffled though, what happened to Cecil. I wasn't called upon to do the honours for him too, so assume he lived a long and happy satisfying life elsewhere. Doubt very much that he would still be walking around alive somewhere today."

Arthur passed over in the 1930's, before the outbreak of the 2nd world war. "Can't remember the exact date I popped me clogs. Probably around 1936, I would guess. But as you know, these dates are meaningless when one is here, eh?"

"Yes, that is how I feel now," I said. "As if all the things which seemed important in the past are so trivial now. Almost like we all lived our lives in fear of nothing. It could seem almost pointless and depressing. But obviously, there is a greater reason for it all," I lamented.

"But you're not depressed, Lass!" he stated.

"No Arthur, all seems so beautiful."

"Aye, it does. Maybe that is why we have been chosen to stay."

"There are others too, though? Other ghosts?"

"Yes there are. Not all as nice as us. Some never even got to that tunnel towards the light. Some refused to go into it in the first place, like the Devilish Pope."

"Devilish Pope?"

"Yes, that is what I call him. Spouts religious nonsense in Latin. He is an old ghost. I knew of him when I was alive. He haunted hereabouts and this cottage that I and Reeney lived in. Lots of people saw him. All dark and hunched. Some called him 'The Priest'. I learnt Latin at school - very useful and necessary to become a doctor in my time. But he spouts religious gibberish, in Latin, about satanic witchcraft and exorcising the world of unbelievers. A bit ironic when you think that someone should exorcise him. But you'll know what I mean if you meet him."

"You lived here then?"

"Aye, Lass. Used to be a place of laughter away from the cares of the world. It was a bright place, full of love. Not the shambling wreck you now see it as. It was just what I needed. As a Doctor, it was remote enough for me to take my jacket off, roll my sleeves up and let my hair down. Of course, that is when I had hair," he chuckled and appeared to stroke his balding head. "Yes, I needed a place out of town. Somewhere just remote enough that people don't knock on your door at teatime, telling you about their ailments. Piles and the such-like." He added, "Just what you don't need at teatime! But not so far, if you were needed, to deliver a young whelp into the world. Been a number of owners since then, and the last lot were a shambles who dinnae deserve the place."

Arthur made a motion of pointing his pipe and seemed as if lightly spitting a strand of tobacco from his mouth in disgust at the memory.

"We have three ghosts. Tilly, whom I also call Tinker. She is harmless. A young girl about 6 years old. Victorian. You'll see her sometime. Just rushes about the place, occasionally knocking things over and filling the place with laughter. Then there is Edward, the young farm lad. He is shy as can be, so it may take a while until he presents himself to you. Kicked in the head by a horse when he was around 15, about 1910. Probably lucky at that. He missed the horrors of the Great War." Then as an aside he stated, "Not that death, as we know, is that bad, but the agony of dying or disfigurement and grief can seem unbearable for the living. And there was plenty of that in the Great War." After a pause, he continued, "Then there is, as I said, the one I call, the Devilish Pope an evil entity who seems to hate anything. He is the one to watch out for. Especially, seems to hate women, so best be on your guard."

"But he can't physically hurt me?"

"No, Lass. Nothing can touch you physically unless you want it to. But he is an ancient ghost. He has been here for a few hundred years I would guess. He has learnt all the tricks and ways of what is possible for a ghost to do, that I know. But he knows a lot more than I do. If he could sap your energy and turn you to dust - he would do it in an instant!" Arthur clapped his hands together, to emphasise this point, and puffed harder on the pipe, which hung from his mouth.

"He could sap my energy?"

"He would try to. He is greedy for energy, so he is!"

We had moved from what must have once been the living room and were sitting side by side on an old oak bench, a bit like a church pew, which lined one wall of the dilapidated kitchen area. A huge Aga oven with hobs faced us. Two rusted kettles and a saucepan still sat on top. The seat was probably a settle where the previous owners sat to warm themselves by the fire on winter nights. Unopened tins of food littered the area, along with unwashed dishes and saucepans which had turned mouldy, and the latter also beginning to rust. A few of the cupboard doors hung on their hinges. Insects and other creatures flashed around the area, going about their business. I detected a rat, scurrying behind the oven, making a bit of noise as he went. I almost felt a warm, smile-like glow come over my manifestation. I thought about how this all would have horrified and disgusted me during life. Now I understood it to be just living creatures using the resources at their disposal to go forward with their own lives. There was no evil intent on their part towards the living - or us *non living creatures*. Some fed on others, but it was just as it was, survival.

"So what is this energy? Do I need to eat to get it as in life?"

"No Lass, no. We canna eat as such." Arthur appeared to puff harder on his pipe as if he were looking for the words to simplify things for me. "As we walk around we pick up energy from the living creatures around us. They share some of that energy, as a form of tax - so to speak. You might have noticed how they change and alter colour as you pass them by."

I nodded.

"But, entities like the Devilish Pope - Poltergeist, or demonic spirits, you could say, well, they try to take more energy than is given. If you give them half the chance, they will sap energy from you too. That is why you must always stay strong and not let down your guard when they are around. Always remember that 'He' has not the ability to hurt you if you don't let him."

"When does this Devilish Pope come around here? Are there warning signs?"

"Often as not when people are here. He likes to feed off their energy. Most people have so much excess energy they never use," he remarked.

My manifestation gave an involuntary shudder. Arthur noticed this. He removed his pipe and said, "They scare you, don't they Lass, the living, I mean?"

"Yes - but I don't know why. Am I afraid they will see me dead? Am I afraid that I will miss being alive and start to regret my passing, even though I know it was the most natural thing to happen?"

"No Angela!" he had used my living name. "No, it probably isn't for those reasons. What I have learnt is that living people scare the living creatures of nature which exist around us. Their lights tend to flicker differently when people approach the building or enter.

"The animals, and insects, are afraid because the living have so much power to control the elements of life. They can, on a whim it seems, chop down trees, on which the creatures of nature depend for their livelihoods. They could even burn this house down, which feeds them so well. The living, by that I mean "People", can be so reckless and thoughtless. We, as ghosts, so to speak, are very sensitive to this fear. In a way, we vicariously manifest that fear ourselves because we pick it up from those around us. It is something you will need to try to overcome. We can absorb some of that energy from people too. This then allows us to carry on for longer, and stronger, to achieve whatever it is we were sent to do. As for the Living seeing you, that can only happen if you manifest yourself to them. And my girl, that takes a lot of energy to do and requires them to be open to seeing you in the first place. Occasionally it may happen by accident. But it is a rare set of circumstances to bring that about."

I thought about this new information. "So even in death, there are still some fears I have to overcome? I thought that was all done with! And what have we been sent back to do? I haven't been told yet. Are we supposed to know?"

"So many questions. So many, only to be expected," Arthur waved his pipe in the air and the smell of tobacco smoke grew stronger. It was a comforting smell because it was Arthur's smell. I trusted Arthur and he was helping me make sense of what was what. This surreal situation I now found myself in.

"For one thing Lass, I have been here and abouts' for almost 60 years, and I am still not truly sure why I am here. I just know... know, that it is correct and that I am needed here. I have a few suspicions but wouldn't want to share these unless they sour the pitch. Alter the way things should be. Best I keep Shtum on that. As for why you are here, what your purpose may be? - I wouldn't know. When will you know? It could be in the next moment - or it could be years. But may I just ask you, Lass, what do you remember about your passing?"

"I remember being above my body, looking down, then the tunnel, the light, the voices. Oh, and for a brief moment, I remembered hundreds of past lives, lives through history, and some drab and other exotic locations, some harsh times, and thousands of successes and failures as a massive rush. Like I have always been, and always will be and that none of my past lives were in vain. They all had a point, the loves, laughter, grief, despair and tragedy. And then, that was suddenly closed off to me and I was back here. But it was years later. Even though it had only seemed like moments I had been away, and this house was altered!"

"All of that is correct, I believe we have had hundreds - if not thousands of lives! We have been around since time began."

"If that is so why can't we access all the experience and voices from the past? Wouldn't that make us stronger? Stronger than the Devilish Pope even? We could reach back farther than him and be more powerful if we needed to. Wouldn't that make more sense?"

"Possibly, Lass. But maybe that would be too confusing too. Maybe in a way, all of those 'before' lives have been sifted through to create what you became in your last life. Maybe you can, without even knowing it, draw on the strength from those lives if need be. It has honed your instincts. Maybe, you are the best to deal with the tasks ahead. And yet, maybe all those other lives would distract you from your task. Who knows?"

I thought for a moment. So glad to have Arthur's clarity and wisdom on the matter. I felt so sure that what he said was probably right. This comforted me a lot.

"But Lass, what do you remember about 'How' you came to pass?"

"How?" I was puzzled, "I am not sure." I couldn't think straight and a surge of panic I never expected sent off vibes of energy around me. A cupboard door blew shut and a tin can heavily fell from a shelf, hitting the floor with a crash. I was startled, "How Arthur, how did I pass, why can't I remember? Do you know?"

"Steady, Lass, easy now. Calm yourself." He tried to reassure me by putting his hand on my arm. I realised what he was doing and manifested, acceptance of his touch to my right forearm. He patted it and stroked it to soothe me. "Aye, Lass. I'll not lie, I saw your passing. But it is not for me to tell you how it happened. Such a pretty Lass you were in life, such a shame!"

This last comment made me sit up. I stopped the manifestation of my arm immediately. Arthur's reassuring hand went through me and fell back to his knee. For an instant I wondered, was Arthur somehow connected to my passing? Was he to blame? Then I thought better. From what I had learnt so far, there was no blame for the living or the dead. What happened, happened. But, I also thought, does that include a ghost's actions? If Arthur had been involved in my 'Death' somehow, was that appropriate? I was momentarily confused and exhausted at the same time.

"I feel tired now - rather lacking energy. I can't think straight. I think that I should go upstairs to one of the bedrooms and be alone for a while."

"Aye, Lass, that would probably be best. Keep your strength up. We can chat later." I nodded, and in an instant, I was alone in a room upstairs which I had remembered and visualised, thankful that I hadn't had to walk the stairs. One of the better-decorated rooms, decorated with blue wallpaper. Only a bit of ivy growing in through a broken pane in the window. Layers of dust across the furniture. I lay on the bed and shut myself off. Not sleep exactly, just a quietness of soul and the comfort of darkness.

I had a lot to settle in my thoughts, and now also a niggling doubt as to the sincerity of Arthur. Why was he here, without fully passing over and why had he not been shown his true mission in all these years? Was he - like the Devilish Pope, a negative force? Did he have something to do with my passing? And yet there was something about him that I felt deep inside to be warm and positive. Something in my instincts told me to trust him.

I powered down my energy and rested.

Chapter 3

On Love and Laughter (what is precious as opposed to what really doesn't matter)

A few days later, Spring was in the air. The peeling wallpaper and moth-eaten net curtains of the blue bedroom were gently moving occasionally in the warm light breeze. I sat with Tilly on the floor as we flicked through a book she had found in the loft. It was one of her favourite books. She had probably read it a thousand times at least. Though how much longer it would last in the damp conditions I wouldn't like to say. Mould already covered the front and back cover boards, and the pages were crumbling at the edges.

Her laughter was infectious. We had taken to each other almost immediately. "Are you my new Mother?" she had asked me on a couple of occasions already. This was slightly bittersweet as I realised that I had never had the chance to have children in my 'last life'. I had been in love with someone and that had lasted almost two years, but sadly had ended. Because of his job, he had been abroad a lot and I suppose this was one of the reasons the relationship ended. How I had dreamed of us being married and having children in the future! But it was never meant to be. Maybe I had come back to be Tilly's mother? I wondered. The thought entered my head but I dismissed the idea. Ridiculous in some ways. I mean when you actually thought about it, Tilly was old enough to be

MY Great, Great, Grandmother. No - that couldn't be the reason I was still here. And, when I thought hard enough about it I could not in the world fathom why a child like Tilly should still be here. Ours is not to reason why, I supposed.

Arthur hadn't been around since we were last in the kitchen together. I wondered where he had wandered off to - another part of the house for some downtime possibly - but I felt sure that he wasn't that close as I couldn't sense his presence. For some reason I felt sure that I would sense him if he was in the house. I sensed someone else, but that presence was younger, so I guess it was the boy that Arthur had mentioned - the farmhand Edward. He was avoiding me, but I felt that he had gotten closer a few times. As if he was curious as to what Tilly and I were up to; I felt he was lonely and wanted to join in the laughter. Without a question between us, Tilly looked up and said, "Yes, that is Edward. He is shy."

Then she started calling, "Shy Boy, Shy Boy, Shy Boy Eddy," as if it were a rhyme. Following this she called, "Edward, don't be a Scaredy-Cat, she is nice. She is gonna be my new Mama!"

We heard a sudden noise. A clinking sound. The atmosphere turned dark as if the creatures had changed colour to deep greys, sour yellows and dull greens, and Tilly's head shot up and she listened intently.

"What is it?' I asked. "Is Edward coming and he is afraid of me?" suddenly feeling afraid.

Tilly, "Shushed!" me.

After a moment she whispered, "It is people."

I wanted to run and hide. "Shall we go to the loft?" I asked, and immediately felt ashamed that in my fear I was asking a six-year-old for advice. But then I remembered,

Tilly wasn't six. She had been doing this for a hundred years or more. She was the best person to advise me.

Tilly suddenly relaxed a bit, rolled over and started looking at her book again, unconcerned. "It's OK! It is only Suhaib. He found the dead boy."

Rather than reassure me, this information posed more questions than answers. I felt at a loss. Then I noticed something else. The smell of tobacco smoke filled the room.

"Hello, Grandpa Arthur," said Tilly.

"Arthur," I called out, fear still in my voice. "Arthur is that you? What is going on? Who is outside, who is Suhaib? What is - was - the dead boy?"

"Easy, Lass," whispered Arthur, "calm yourself. Suhaib is only the security guy. Interesting fellow, used to be a policeman you know. Some sort of scandal and he was out on his ear. Ended up going around places like this these days, and checking they are OK. Supposed to be security, but has never caught anybody here. Though lots have come and gone in between."

"Who was the dead boy?" I worriedly asked again.

"Oh him? Nice lad - but led astray a bit. I tried to warn him. Came with a bunch of older kids once and they all started taking medications, and drugs, to get off their heads. Unfortunately, his body wasn't that strong and he passed. The other kids scattered and left him there after they discovered what had happened. Suhaib found him. Bit of a Hoo-Hah really. Police were here for about a week. Dusting the place for prints etc.," Arthur explained. "As if this place needs any more dust, eh Lass?" he chortled.

"That is terrible," I said and followed up with the question, "is he a ghost here too?"

"Him? ...oh no, he passed straight over. Wouldn't be surprised if his soul was sent straight back to be reborn as a creature. He could be one of the billions of insects in the world - or our kitchen rat even. That is what, I have heard, happens to souls of those who pass after addiction and other misdemeanours."

"How terrible!" I repeated, trying to absorb this new information Arthur had imparted. And then, I realised, that it wasn't terrible. It was natural. Sort of like the theory of evolution. What doesn't survive in nature doesn't go forward to the next level. This young boy's life - his soul - was still energy. It still existed. It just had to be sent back a couple of paces. Like a game of Snakes and Ladders. It was all a natural process. Life keeps pushing forward. Finding gaps in concrete to shoot through and grow. This was how it was. I don't know how, but I just knew this. Something from my awakening. My passing over. I no longer thought like I used to. Death was no longer something to be afraid of. It was like we were on some eternal learning curve. All the souls in the Universes, shooting forward, like rays from the sun, shooting towards the ultimate goal. Some got reflected backwards - but never really died. Back, back, until they were ready to go forward again. Arthur nodded slowly - as if he could read my thoughts. And I knew that what I thought was mostly correct.

"Do we need to hide?" I asked him.

"No, we'll be alright. Suhaib will just have a wander 'round. Look in a couple of windows, check the fences for holes etc. He will only be here about 20 minutes," he reassured me. "It is who he brings with him, that can be a problem sometimes."

"Who he brings?"

"Yes. Don't suppose the job pays much and there is a constant turn-over of his 'deputies', you could say, if one thought of him in terms of the local Sheriff. One fellow, he brought 'round once came back later on his own and tried to steal some of the stuff from here. We frightened him off though. Or rather, Tilly scared him off, didn't you Tinker?"

Tilly looked up from the book and manifested a cheeky grin. Arthur winked back at her.

Arthur was right. Suhaib only spent about 20 minutes outside. Satisfied that all was as should be - he left with his unenthusiastic, young 'deputy', who had remained, looking ever so bored, outside the fenced enclosure, by the security car, with his hands in his pockets. Arthur and Tilly had gone downstairs for a moment, to get some of the energy from the two living entities. I was too afraid to do that. I did, however, manage to peek out of the upstairs window and look at Suhaib and the young man beyond the fence. And, it seemed as if for an instant Suhaib had sensed my presence, he turned and looked up, making me recoil from the window. The net curtains moved. Suhaib looked hard. And, behind the wall, hidden in the room I hoped that he would put the movement of the curtains down to the wind.

Chapter 4

Restrictions and Freedom
of the Machine

A couple of days later I felt like I had been on a permanent boot-camp and Arthur was my Sergeant-Major. His never-ending instructions were educating me and giving me direction. Not by breaking me down and rebuilding me, as modern education does, but by gently nudging me through the process of re-birth I was going through.

We were in the cellar. An interesting place which I warmed to. Not that it was cleaner than another part of the building, but it did have some interesting things, and the floor was in good condition.

Arthur was explaining, "Think of it as if your soul was you - which it is - I know. But your body - that is not you!"

"So I am my soul - but not my body?"

"Yes, that is sort of correct," he replied.

To define it further, he explained, "Your soul is you and your body is like, like, an auto mobile."

"What - I am like a car?"

"Not exactly." He puffed harder on his pipe and frowned. "Your soul goes from place to place, but sometimes it drives a different auto mobile. I dislike the term 'CAR', even though it has its origins in the Celtic, from the word 'carrus', horse before the cart and all that! It seems such a lazy, slap-dash sort of word. I prefer 'Auto-mobile'," he said in an angst voice. "I know it shouldn't matter - but it does. Just put that down to me being an old fogey!"

"OK, ... auto mobile," I repeated but not with enthusiasm.

After a few moments of him staring at me to make sure that I wasn't making fun, he went on.

"Well, if you are you, then 'you' can do anything and go anywhere. Am I making myself clear?" he asked.

"Yes, Aye Aye, Capitan, perfectly clear," I cheekily replied.

He gave me a sardonic look. After a pause he said, "Well in a 'Car', your word - not mine, we are restricted."

"Restricted," I repeated.

"You understand?" he asked - looking uncertain that I was wise enough to follow his argument.

I smiled at him. He tapped his pipe on the fire place in frustration and continued. "Right, well, in an auto-mobile, you have to follow the rules of the road."

"Follow the rules of the road," I repeated.

"Yes, Goddammit, in an auto-mobile, you can't just drive willy-nilly. Turning left or right as you think fit. Dashing off across a piece of moorland because the whim takes you. You have to stick to the road, watch the speed limit... obey the signs!"

"Obey the signs," I repeated, but felt I was losing the thread of the argument and wanted to be elsewhere.

"Yes, my Lass! Obey the signs!"

I looked at him nonplussed.

"Look," he fumed. Frustration was manifest in the demeanour he presented. "Our souls are us – what's inside, our Humanity. And Our Bodies - well, they... they are what we drive in to get around."

After a moment, "Understand, Lass?"

"If I get what you are trying to say, Arthur, then, we could be anyone - anyone as a soul, but we could be born into a prince's body. Is that correct?"

"Yes, my girl, now you are getting it." Arthur seemed to expand, "You may once have been born a child, from the Ghettos of Istanbul, but be reborn in the body, 'automobile body', of the King of Siam."

"Constantinople," I cheekily remarked.

"Whatever," he replied.

"And it is Thailand now, not Siam!" I remarked.

"Whatever, twice," he replied and puffed even harder and longer on his pipe, eyeing me with a frustrated, quizzical look with one eyebrow significantly higher than the other.

"So, if I understand correctly: we are born into a body created by some living people and we bring the wisdom of our souls and these are combined with the inheritance of the blood-line. Is that right?"

"Yes, that is it exactly," he pointed the stem of the pipe at me as an emphasis. He continued, "But, also, when we are alive, our bodies restrict us doing what we could previously as souls do. We can no longer waft around, as we please, re-appear somewhere else miles away in an instant. It is as if we have been made to wear leaden divers' boots. We are restricted. But, by that restriction, comes insights. Insights into matter and the physical realm. We learn to understand and manipulate that matter in a way we never could if we had been wafting souls. Going willy-nilly above the world. We learn how to be. We learn how to interact and improvise. To struggle, to get through with limitations!"

"Okay, I understand now. It is better that it has been explained to me." I was no longer being cheeky or sarcastic, but now I focused more as I understood.

"What about poltergeist, like the Devilish Pope? They can move things around, so are they part auto-mobile still?"

"Well, not really. They have left their bodies but have decided to not to leave this realm. They have never passed over fully. They are like us, but not like us. You, Angela, you have shown that you too could be a poltergeist. I could, if I wished. Do you remember when we were sitting in the kitchen and you made the cupboard slam and something fall off the shelf? Well, that was a sudden release of energy but undirected. Poltergeist, like our Devilish Pope, have been wandering around for years learning what they can do with energy forces. They know how to control it better than we do. Rather than a wave of emotional energy, they go around stacking chairs, throwing things directly at people etc. They are like psychopaths who direct the energy of their anger and frustration, at us and the living. They are in purgatory but don't realise it. They wallow in self-pity, resentment, hate and eagerness for revenge," he explained.

"It's a pity we can't get a tame one in here to tidy up the place. It could do with some dusting and new net curtains, bit of a spring clean," I joked.

Arthur looked sternly at me and said, "Never joke about them, my Lass. It could backfire if you summon one!"

I heeded this warning and then, after a reflective pause, went on.

"But we don't have the memories of our lives previous to our last one. Why not? That would probably help us. We wouldn't make the same mistakes again. And we would have all of that experience to call upon. Almost like demi-gods. Why don't we retain these memories?"

"No, no, that would be too messy, Lass. Too much interference. We would be forever looking back. Mopping about past loves. Searching through antiquarian shops for our old possessions. No, we start again, with pretty much a clean slate. Though," he paused, "occasionally, a mere snippet of the past pops through. Could be from the soul, or from the make-up of the body we've come into. Déjà vu, it is often called, or something similar. But, mainly, we are running on instincts. Fresh start. And anyhow, you should have realised when you passed over. Mistakes are good for us. They are a learning curve. They are never the same mistakes. They may be similar, but the context changes. And, invariably, we hurt ourselves more than others, from the mistakes we make."

"So, when we are 'ALIVE', we are restricted physically? And when we are dead, we aren't restricted physically, but we have little true understanding of the physics of things?"

"Sort of," Arthur was relieved that I had finally gotten part of the concept. "You can move things around, as I explained. However, in an often uncontrolled, emotional exchange of energy. It would be difficult to become say, a blacksmith or a jeweller. That would require too much emotional energy which would be hard to sustain and drain you constantly.

"When you are alive - it is like you are in a body - which is the auto-mobile - which, can interact with the surrounding matter. However, the restrictions mean that you have to also follow certain rules. When you are dead though - you are free to go anywhere, waft anywhere, as far as your energy can take you. There are benefits to both I suppose."

"But poltergeist have the upper-hand because they can manipulate the energy better to stack chairs and such?"

"You could say that. Far worse though is their ability to enter and possess a living person with ease. Then you have a ghost, as such, able to disguise themselves, walk amongst others and manipulate the physical world."

"Could we do that too?"

"Yes, my girl. However, I wouldn't advise it. If you take on the ways of the demon, you are in danger of becoming one yourself. If you ever feel the necessity of doing that then do it because it has to be done. Do it for the shortest time possible. Make sure that the reasons you are doing it align with your destiny."

"What about sins? When I passed, I had no sense of a divine presence. No angels playing harps, sitting on fluffy clouds. I would've hoped that I would have been told what the correct religion was. Instead, I felt that we were all part of the same. We were all part of 'God'. Just one big energy which goes on and on, if that makes sense?"

"Yes, yes," agreed Arthur, waving his pipe around in the air. "Religion is pretty much a man-made construct too. A set of guidelines, like the highway code. Helps some though. When I was a Doctor I sat by many patients who swore that it was their 'God' who got them through the pain, or grief of missing a loved one."

"Also, starts a lot of wars too!"

Arthur stared at me for a few moments before nodding, slowly, as in thought. "Yes, but that isn't the point of our chat today, young lady. Let's get back on track."

"Oh, oh, I just remembered!" I shouted excitedly, "My boyfriend," (the one I really loved - came in my thoughts - and Arthur picked up on these thoughts), "he once said that in his job they had to drive a number of vehicles across an area and that they had 'Governors' fitted to the engines. He said that these 'Governors' restricted the speed to 40mph. But his driver removed his - and that meant they could go a lot faster - then that caused a lot of problems for my boyfriend in the end. Is that similar?"

"Yes, though I am not sure I get 100% what you are trying to explain. But the human body is like a soul with 'Governors' fitted. These restrict what you do in life, what you see and how much you can sense ...and then, we are further restricted by our level - or lack of belief!"

"What belief in religion, I am still confused. I thought that religion was only guidelines. So, the Devilish Pope, he still believes – though he has passed - like us. Doesn't he know that it is gobble-die-gook?"

"No, don't go back to that again!" he said, as if vexed. "Nothing to do with religion. Those are man-made constructs! The Devilish Pope, he never completely passed and so he is stuck in his own fog of religious mania. He uses the pieces of religion that the hypocrites of the Spanish Inquisition most likely adhered to. Nothing to do with love and goodness in all. Some people just weaponise religion for their own ends, and he is certainly one of those!"

He went on, "The beliefs I am talking about are more to do with the belief that each individual has in themselves and the vehicle, auto-mobile, car - they have been allocated to drive. Believe me, when I say that, almost anything is possible. If you want to believe in yourself to do it, and what you want to do is defined in the parameters of what you have been dealt, then you can do it, if you truly wish. The last people who lived here used to have that television contraption on all the time. I often saw the news. People, climbing mountains with artificial limbs, and all that. Unheard of in my day. When soldiers came back from the war they were lucky if somebody carved them a stump for their missing leg. Didn't have all of these modern artificial limbs which could pass for the real thing. Next they'll be putting a Man on Mars before you know it!"

"Or Woman," I cheekily remarked. "And that is, if you actually believe that we have already put someone on the moon, in the first place."

"Oh, bit of a cynic, are we? And yes – woman. Let's say person. Damn semantics! Excuse my temper. I do find you, sometimes, slightly more vexatious to deal with than young Edward, or Tilly, Lass."

I gave him a cheeky grin and asked, "The young Edward and Tilly who are both years older than the both of us?"

He smiled and shook his head from side to side as if he despaired of me.

"Right, where were we?" He scratched his bald head.

"As a thought. Can we change the name of the Devilish Pope to something simpler? Like Devlin? It'd be easier to say!" I pushed in on the conversation.

"What? Why change it? Is that some Americanisation?" He looked perplexed.

"Well, you said it was the name you called him and that he had also been known as 'The Priest', didn't you? So, I was thinking that maybe he wasn't a Priest in reality anyway. And, I also thought that giving him the Pope status may give into his ego. Anyway, Devlin is an Irish name I believe. I used to know a fireman, who was a friend of my Dad's called Devlin."

"Just because you knew a stoker on a steam train called Devlin, doesn't mean that you can come in here after only 5 minutes and change all and sundry around, my girl."

"Not a stoker of a steam train. He was a fireman – in the Fire Brigade. Big hats, hoses, axe, and climbs ladders to rescue people and put out fires. We don't have steam trains any more. Unless, you want to go to some touristy place where they have been preserved."

"Oh, confound it all and damnation. Have your way, Lass, change his name as you like. I wouldn't want to confound your grey matter by using two words where you could use one!"

"Thank you, Grandpa!" I used the name that Tilly had used. It did the trick and seemed to soften him up.

"Oh, fiddle-sticks!" he said. "I feel I don't have the energy to go on further today. I am going to power-down for a while in a dark-room – that is unless your Ladyship would like to change anything else at present?"

"No, that will do for now. Thank you for your help, 'Grandpa'."

"Right you are, then. We can continue tomorrow. And when I come back I don't want to find all the furniture moved around, the place dusted and net curtains put up. Do you hear me? I am fond of things just how they are!"

"Yes Sir," I saluted with a big smile splitting my face from ear to manifested ear.

He gave me a look of despair. "How old were you when you passed?"

I remained to attention and snapped back, "Twenty five, I believe, Sir."

"A jolly person you are, I am sure. But lacking somewhat in the maturity department, I think!" he said, shaking his head.

He gruffed a cough, and left.

Chapter 5

Sins of the Flesh

Arthur, came bouncing into the lounge, whilst I had Tilly on my lap. We had been reading another book and Tilly was getting restless. Tilly, looked up, "Mama, I am going outside to play," she told me.

"OK, darling but be careful out there that you don't trip up," suddenly, realising that I had quickly fallen into the role she had designated me and that it was very unlikely a ghost would ever trip over either.

"I will be careful, Mama," she answered and skipped out though the doors leading to the veranda.

"Bye, Granpa," she called to Arthur as she left.

"Bye, bye my dear," he responded.

He then turned and addressed me.

"Have you thought about anything you might want to ask me since yesterday?"

"Yes, a few things have crossed my mind. You said that people come here sometimes. Who, and when? Were you just talking about those youngsters and Suhaib? Or are there others?"

"Well, as you will meet them I'd better forewarn you. It isn't just Suhaib, or those youngsters. They come occasionally – or others like them – but they tend to keep their distance now. I think they believe the place is haunted. Though why they should, I have no idea," he winked. "Sometimes they just throw a rock or two at the windows like cowardly hoodlums."

He went on, "The ones who come regularly, well, there are the Lovers, and the Ghost Explorers – as they call themselves."

"Ohh Arrr... Lovers. That sounds exciting." I sat up on the sofa on my knees, in anticipation that Arthur would elaborate.

"Oh, and there is that artist fellow, too - Josh - shouldn't forget him. He just sits and sketches. A quiet fellow, harmless enough."

"That's interesting, but tell me more about the lovers. They sound slightly more interesting. Are they a young courting couple?"

"Young? No, I should coco! They are in their 30's and married."

"Married?" I asked, disappointed. I felt cheated, "Well, that isn't what I would hardly call 'Lovers', an old married couple."

"You miss my point, my dear," he said condescendingly. "They are married. But not to each other. They meet here for their secret liaisons. Away from their respective spouses. She is a strange woman with strange desires."

"Oh Arrrh!" I couldn't stop myself again, from expressing my interest.

"But, that can't be wrong can it? I mean, when you pass, you find that what we were brought up to believe was 'wrong', was mostly incorrect. It's all made up rules just to keep the peace. I wish I had done some more love-making!" (I used this term as respect for Arthur's age and persona). "When I was alive. I was a very good girl by modern standards. I only had one lover, and I was fully in love with him at the time," I gushed out.

"Well, anyway, you will see them, but probably I shouldn't talk too much to a young lady like you about these things."

"Oh, Arthur, you can't just put the cork back in the bottle. Now you have started telling me about this you have to go on and finish. Anyway, it won't affect me, I haven't thought much about that sort of thing since I passed."

"Well, you wouldn't, my girl. We ghosts don't get much of an urge for hanky-panky. When you think about it, the urge to make merry," (I almost laughed when I heard him say this but didn't want to upset him in mid-flow) "this urge, mostly comes from the need to produce children. That doesn't apply to ghosts, or for those before puberty. You could say that we have returned to a state of innocence."

"So what do this couple of 'Lovers' get up to then?"

"Well, if I was to say the term 'Slap and Tickle', with these two – it tends to be more slap than tickle. If you get my drift?"

"Oh, bondage sort of thing?" I asked, and Arthur's eyes almost popped out of his manifested eye sockets when I said this.

"Wherever did you get such a word, my girl?" he asked. "Really, you quite surprise me sometimes with the things you come out with. But, I'm not sure that that is the right description. She never gets tied up, but she does like him to hit her sometimes."

"So, he is a bit of a brute?" I was attempting to keep my language to terms that Arthur would probably more readily find acceptable.

"Well, that's the queerest thing. Sometimes, it is him that just wants to get on with the love-making, and it is her that encourages him to be rough. She actively encourages him. I think it isn't fully his cup of tea, and he would rather get on with it. Probably helps by coming to a place like this, out-of-the-way as it is. No one able to hear her screams and other, er, noises."

"Well, I think that smacking someone is wrong," I said.

Arthur thought a moment. "Mm... not always," he said.

"What do you mean?" I asked him.

"Well when it is a deterrent to greater wrongs it is not always a bad thing," he stated. "Like bringing up children, there has to be some way of disciplining them."

"I don't agree, Arthur. I don't believe in violence," I said.

"I am not talking about lashing out, Angela. I am talking about punishment to deter a greater hurt."

"Well I don't agree, especially in lashing out at children. It could mentally scar them for life. I think that the differences in the eras we lived through shows how our opinions can alter over time. I believe that the human race has grown in understanding since your generation."

"Oh, you really believe that eh, girl? Maybe in your cushioned world things have changed. But not everywhere. There are some countries with people who live through worse hardships than we can imagine. They are not fortunate enough to be able to live within the realms of your ideals, I am afraid. If it came to a contest between this country and theirs, well, they'd eat us for breakfast. We have grown soft, so we have."

"Anyway, my children turned out alright," Arthur said. "They were two young strong bucks who got up to all sorts of mischievous activities. Irene and me – well we couldn't be with them all hours of the day – we had too much to be getting on with. Anyway, it isn't just about the smack, or spanking that you need to consider."

"What is it about then rather than the threat of physical violence as punishment?"

"It is about the wait in between, that is the point," he stated. I looked at him puzzled.

"Look, when our lads got into trouble, I don't know, when one of them had broken a window, or had taken something from the neighbouring farms. Reeney would say to them, 'now you just wait till your father gets home'. And they would plead with her to not tell me. But she was having none of it. She knew, like I did, that if they got away with it then they would think they could do it again – or worse. And that would lead to greater trouble for them."

"So, hitting them would stop that, would it?" I asked, slightly sneering in turn. I was beginning to doubt that Arthur was as wise as I thought he was. He really hadn't kept up with the times.

"No," he agreed. "Hitting them doesn't stop them. It's the 'wait' that stops them." He put his shoulders back and looked at me.

"The wait? What do you mean, 'the wait'?" I asked, uncertainly.

"I mean the time between when Reeney said that to them, and the time I got home. The 'wait' is, when they would go through in their minds' all the excuses under the sun. They would dwell on what they had done. Sometimes, Irene would telephone me from the house and tell me. She would use a sort of code so that the telephone operator didn't overhear and air our dirty laundry in public. She would say, 'The foxes have been worrying the chickens again'. I knew what that meant. Those times I would delay coming home. I would go into one of the local pubs and have a jaw with the farmers. That wait would drag out. It would become excruciating for the lads. They knew that I hardly would ever hit them that much when I got back. Just a slap of the slipper on the backside to give them closure. But by then, their imagination of the punishment had turned it into a massive beating, from which, they would just survive with their lives."

I interrupted him, "So it was about mental torture as well as physical punishment, then?"

"Not at all, Lass. Their conscience would be like an over-ripe plum, ready to explode. They would finally make up THEIR OWN MINDS, that what they had done was wrong. Instead of excuses they would be at the stage to apologise and promise never to do it again. Teachers used to know the same thing when they threatened the cane. You won't have had it happen to you, but in my day, when you were told to go wait outside the headmaster's office, you were made to wait, and wait, and wait. It stops a lot of hurt in the end and teaches people how to grow up to police themselves. Self-control and all that! If you had a child who you never threatened with some form of punishment, then they would never feel that there were consequences for their actions. There would be anarchy all over and they would hurt themselves in the process. It is only done because you love them and you don't want greater harm to befall them later."

I sort of saw what Arthur meant, as discipline in schools had become chaotic and ineffective, it seemed. However, I told him that I didn't fully agree with him and that if I had had children, I would have loved them and never threatened them."

"Whatever," he said, "we can agree to disagree, on this."

"Anyway, getting back to this thing with the 'Lovers' and their consensual 'kinky' practices," he said, "there is one good thing about it all."

"What's that?" I knew he wanted me to ask.

"They give off lots and lots of energy in the process."

"So, you absorb that energy? Aren't you afraid it is contaminated or something?"

"No, good lord, no. Energy is energy. It is neither good nor bad. It is the user who uses it for good or evil. We all take some of that energy, me, Tilly and even Edward, will sometimes sneak into the back of the room."

"NO!" I felt myself scream out, "you can't tell me that you encourage two children to join you in watching a couple of kinky lovers?" I was flabbergasted.

"No, no – don't get me wrong, my girl!" he said defensively, "We don't sit and watch, we just get to a position where we can absorb the energy. Tilly takes no notice of them herself. Having never reached puberty, I am not sure she has the faintest idea what is going on. The best way to describe it would be to think of it as lying in the park, on a warm sunny, summer's day and feeling the rays of the sun on your body. Excepting the noise, that is. Tremendous energy they give out in their exertions, so they do."

"Well, maybe it is because I have recently passed that I find this so horribly wrong," I stated.

"In time you will come to understand. Try to think of it as two auto-mobiles, or 'cars', grinding together. Then it may seem more amusing than threatening. It is just two people taking their vehicles for a test drive."

"But why? Why all the kinky stuff? Why, aren't the living satisfied with doing 'it' for love and for reproducing?" On reflection, even I thought this question to be slightly prudish and judgemental, but I had asked it.

Arthur just stared at me. He paused and then continued, waving his pipe in the air.

"A lot of 'whys' you asked there. And I suppose that that is the biggest unanswered question in life, 'Why?' And, as it turns out, is the most pointless question. It is, because it is! And that is it whenever the word 'why' springs up." He paused and after a moment continued,

"I think, it is just an idea of mine, but I think that it is something in the human nature to try to get to the inner soul. Do you remember that feeling of euphoria you felt when you passed?"

I nodded.

"Well," he went on, "I think that when we are born into a body we hanker after the feeling of power and freedom we have lost by being contained in a body. After all, it can be pretty uncomfortable living as a person. Some hardships are difficult to navigate and there is always that nagging, unanswered question, 'Why?', which never seems to get answered, but is constantly asked. It keeps us on a permanent path to seek the answer. That is all very frustrating for the living!

"Some people find it hard to cope and go to extreme methods to escape the imposed bonds on their souls. They look for answers in what could be considered to be 'the wrong places'. Some drink to excess. I was very fond of the odd tipple myself. Liked a dram of the hard-stuff, whisky, I mean. Others take drugs... like that, that young lad who passed here! And some seek escape through carnal pleasure, so to speak."

I spent a few moments thinking about what he said.

"I don't think my boyfriend found me very exciting in bed," I reflected as I felt a huge wave of regret pass over me. This was the most powerful 'Living-type' emotion I had had since my passing. "Don't get me wrong. I truly believed that he loved me. But he was quite a few steps ahead of me in the love-making department. I just felt that he wanted more and I wanted to go at a slower pace. Which was difficult, because he was always away working and really, we had so little time together when he was back. In the year and a half, plus, we were together we had short spells of ecstatic pleasure, followed by the heartbreak of separation for weeks. A long-distance relationship, so they say. Bit of a roller-coaster relationship really. It was horrible when we finally split up though. I somehow always thought we would end up together, again, in the future. You know, in my heart, I thought we were meant for each other and would one day be married and have kids."

"Nay, nay, Lass. Dinnae punish yourself with regrets about what might have been. You should know that these things are less important now. It is just a process that you'll have to work through, until you accept 'how' you passed."

"My passing again. You're not going to tell me what happened to me, are you Arthur?"

"No, sometimes when things have a lot of trauma attached to them, it is only for the soul themselves to work things out. Me, intervening and giving my interpretation, won't help you on that. When the time is right, the answer will appear. You'll know then – and come to some acceptance."

"Traumatic?" I sat up straight. "Did I fall down the stairs and bang my head?"

"You won't catch me out, that way, my girl. When the time is right, you'll know. And that is the last I am saying on that."

After some quiet, almost reflective time, in which Arthur pretended to smoke and fill the room with the smell of burnt tobacco, I asked, "You said there were others? The artist, oh and the ghost busters? Can you tell me about them, please?"

"Oh, the artist? Young chap, comes in here every now and again, during the daytime, and sits and sketches. Young Tilly and Edward enjoy sitting and watching him. He used to live here, you know. His father was a writer, had this place in the seventies. Young Josh, that's his name - the artist. Lovely family really.

"And Tilly, she was Josh's best friend for years. Right up till he was about seven. They used to sit on the floor and all you would hear was laughter. At first the parents were worried. They even took him to a doctor once, but were told that it was only natural for a youngster to have an 'invisible friend'. Especially being out in the sticks like this, and an only child, to-boot! Sadly though – late 70's I think, his mother passed away, cancer. I was here when she went. Her husband was devastated. Couldn't write so well afterwards. Went downhill a bit. I remember her looking at me as she passed, looking back at her husband and asking me to take care of them both. She was at peace. Then she passed-over. Didn't return as a ghost."

As an aside, I said, "I knew another lad who didn't live that far from here whose mother died when he was young. That is terrible for a young child to grow up without a parent." I mused on this thought for a few moments. And then asked,

"What sort of things did he draw?"

I had always like art as a subject myself. That was something I had in common with the love of my life. We had been down to London and Cambridge a few times to wander around some of the galleries. He had been good at sketching, and I was more into colourful designs and painting. In my day dreaming times I had thought that at one stage – if we did marry, we would bring our children up to be artists. And who knows, we might have ended up painting in our retirement, living in a country cottage. Some place by a babbling brook. Silly to look back on it now. Such foolish dreams, so far removed from reality.

"Draw? Oh, all sorts. Sometimes he draws objects from the room, other times some of the trees and plants outside. He also," at this Arthur paused and raised an eyebrow at me, "...has a book of photos of nude people, he takes out of his satchel, and he draws those. Not rude pictures, all quite tastefully done, anatomical studies and the like. Yes, he is skilled. Maybe he comes here because he doesn't want to upset his father at home by that sort of art. Or maybe he comes for the peace and quiet and to remember his mother and the times he had with Tilly. Or just to get away from it all. Even the creatures of nature don't seem to mind him being around. I think they can sense that he means no harm. Only time Tilly ever seems sad though, is because she can't connect with him any more. I suppose children have a ghost-detecting sense that they lose when education is introduced."

"He sounds nice," I said, smiling.

"The only thing he doesn't seem to want to draw is the curtains."

I felt puzzled, and tried to picture whether any of the curtains in the rooms were worth drawing. "Why would he want to draw the curtains?" I asked.

Arthur just stood and gawked at me, holding his pipe forward expectantly.

When I didn't say anything he started to chortle, "It's a joke my dear!"

"Oh, I get it now Arthur, Draw the curtains, oh very funny. A sort of joke my Dad would have come out with,"

I chuckled – more to keep him happy than because of the validity of the joke.

"Sounds like a good man your Father, sort I would get along with. Is he still with us?"

"As far as I know he is," I said, "not sure how long it's been. He seemed healthy enough when I last saw him. It is my Mother who was the frail one."

"You could go and see them," Arthur replied.

I thought about it for a few moments. Somehow, I was reluctant. Almost as if I was to blame for my passing, and that they would feel upset and I would feel guilty. "Probably not best at the moment," I said.

"Whatever, you think is right, my girl. In your own time now," he said compassionately.

Then he turned the subject of the conversation back again.

"And you asked about, what you called, the ghost busters? Well, they are a group of three people who come around here to try to contact us. Bit of a joke if you ask me. They often bring all this equipment with them. Gadgets and what nots, a few cameras, and they film things. Ask a lot of silly questions too. If they are not careful they are going to attract the attention of 'Devlin', as you like to call him. Then they will regret their actions, you mark my words, girl!"

"Do you ever talk to them?"

"What me – communicate? I should say not! I have nothing to tell them that they are not going to learn themselves when the time comes for their passing. That's going to be closer than they know. The living always think that they have the monopoly on life and that these things won't happen to them. They're wasting their short time on this earth, if you ask me. And that equipment, must cost a fortune. They really should get real jobs and do something useful with their time."

"Do you think the artist does something useful with his time?" I asked, and then quickly added, "I am not being facetious or anything. I just want your opinion, Arthur. I mean, is it selfish to want to sit and draw all day? Does it ever do any good, or should we, when living, spend our time like Mother Teresa, helping others?"

"Interesting questions, Lass. I did see that 'Mother Teresa' on that television contraption. A sort of saintly life, you mean? I suppose it was me being 'facetious' when I spoke about the 'Paranormal Seekers', as they like to call themselves. I shouldn't really criticise. Who knows? There may be some purpose in what they do. Maybe the ultimate goal of their searching is to come to a point in the future where we need to communicate betwixt the living and dead realms. Maybe they are a cog-in-the-wheel. Who knows?

"With the art though, I have actually given it some thought. I mean there are people who do things such as meditate, etc. On the face of it – that doesn't produce a lot. I believe that art is a form of meditation too. As least an artist produces a drawing that someone can enjoy from the process though. But with both, meditation and art, I think, 'Yes', they are necessary." Arthur started to pace slowly back and forth in the room. The birds were singing outside. Another warm spring day.

He continued to think aloud, "Not just for therapy for the individual. I mean there is so much violence and destruction in the world. Art and meditation bring a little balance, a little peace to the chaos. If you think about it, young lady, we have probably lived through many wars and upsets in our past lives. Why shouldn't people deserve a little down-time when things are easy? Saying that though, a lot of the greatest art was produced amid conflicts too. I remember after the Great War, going to a few exhibitions of work, from artists who had been there and seen it. Some people would get upset and think that these paintings were either wicked or unpatriotic. But I admired the fact that the human spirit can pull something out of that twisted mess, to try to make sense of it. And the process of meditation and peace which comes from creating something – maybe not just by an artist's hands – but by any skilled craftsman, there is a certain beauty in that!" Arthur stopped pacing and looked at me. It was as if he had gotten something off his chest.

"You were in the Great War too...weren't you Arthur?"

He frowned again. "Yes, my girl, I was," and after a moment's inward reflection he brightly looked up and said, "but we mustn't dwell on that, eh? All in the past, and all that."

He then went onto explain more about the ghost busters (as I liked to call them). Two men, late twenties, and a girl – early twenties. She did most of the filming whilst the other two would prance about the place, trying to get a response to their infernal questions. Always seeking a reaction to electronic devices.

Apparently, they came in and set up, often late afternoon, then returned when it was dark and, as Arthur said, "Went stomping all over the place in their big boots knocking things over and making holes in the floorboards!"

Chapter 6

On Meeting Edward and going outside

It was two days later that I met Edward for the first time. I felt his presence whilst I was in the dining room. It was amazing, in a way, that the furniture was still here. The sideboard with the glasses and some crockery still inside. There were a couple of drawers – one with cutlery, and the other with some personal effects, letters, photos and the such-like. A long oak table with seven seats around it sat in the middle of the large room. I think there should have been eight chairs, but one was probably in another room somewhere. Apart from the peeling wallpaper in places, the room was still pleasant to sit in.

Edward popped his head around the door. "Hello Miss, didn't mean to intrude, but is it alright to come in for a bit?"

I greeted him warmly, "Hello Edward. It is wonderful to meet you. I have heard some lovely things about you."

At this, Edward's eyes went further towards the floor and his whole demeanour manifested what I can only describe as a blush. "Thank you, ma'am," he said shuffling in. He looked extremely uncomfortable in his clothing. As if before he passed over, he had already outgrown his fourteenth year clothes and was ready to fit into a couple of sizes larger to begin his fifteenth year. But he had never had the opportunity.

He sat in the farthest chair he could from me, as if he was afraid I might suddenly bite him. The only thing I really wanted to do though was give him a hug. However, I feel that would probably have made him run for the hills. Therefore, I sat patiently smiling, waiting for him to feel comfortable enough to talk.

"Nice day, Miss."

"Yes, it is, Edward. I think that we have been very fortunate in having such a pleasant spring so far. Some days it has almost been like summer."

"Yes Miss."

"Edward, you don't have to call me Miss. I am not a school teacher you know."

"I know you're not a Teacher, Miss, but I don't know what else to call you Miss!"

"You could call me by my name, Angela, you know."

"Oh, I couldn't do that Miss, that would be over-fimillaar, over-familler, so my mum used to say, Miss."

"Now, that wouldn't be over-familiar, that would be fine. After all, we are practically family. I mean, we live in the same house, don't we?"

"Well, I suppose when you say that Miss, er – I mean, Anj-e-…, Angela, I suppose we are Miss! Though I spend a lot of time outside, Miss. Around the fields out front, and the woods out-a-back. Have you been outside Miss, er Angela? It is nice out there."

"No, I haven't, Edward. Not yet anyway."

"Well I could show you sometime, Miss, when you're ready, of course. I wouldn't like to be too pushy, Arthur wouldn't like me being pushy. All in good time, he would say. But me and Tilly, we love to play in the outdoors. In weather like this it would be nice for you to get out sometimes. Lots of energy about. You don't think I am being too pushy Miss, does yer? I don't mean to be Miss, er, Angela."

"No, I don't think that you are being too pushy Edward. I think that you have a lovely way of asking a girl out!"

Edward immediately braced up in a defensive posture.

"Oh, I didn't mean that Miss. I wasn't asking you out, not in that way. I wouldn't want you to get the wrong 'pression of me Miss. I am not a freshen... not fresh like some other lads. I'm re, re, re- spectful, I am Miss!" he stuttered.

"Oh, Edward, I don't think you were being fresh. I would love to come out to be shown the fields and woods. Just like a member of your family would like to be shown around. Like, say, a cousin, would."

"Yes – that's it, Miss, just like a cousin or sumthing! That's what I meant."

"Well, I am a little nervous about going out, I must admit, but," I sat up straighter, more determined, "but, it's a lovely day. Why don't we go out now, Edward?"

"Now Miss? Oh yes, we could go now if you'd like to. That would be fine. Maybe Tilly is out and about and we could find her an' all go for a walk together?" Edward seemed very pleased, whilst I was happy to start to gain his trust.

Although I couldn't directly feel the warmth of the sun's rays on my face, I did feel a burst of energy as we passed out of the back kitchen door. Outside was a large paved courtyard with various out-buildings, brick-built garages, a barn and lean-to sheds surrounding it. Also, other buildings, part brick and wooden, which I supposed had once stabled horses plus a cart or two, possibly also workshops for maintenance. The house was over 300 years old, Arthur had told me, so I would have thought that a horse and cart would have been essential back-in-the-day. Bits of old cars lay strewn about these outhouses. A dilapidated tow-truck, windows green with moss and weeds growing on it in places where dirt had accumulated over the years. In one lean-to-structure, I could see remnants of what looked like farm implements, various tools and mechanical equipment. All crammed into areas on top of each other. To get to the back of that lot would be virtually impossible I thought. Not organised at all.

We approached a five-bar gate. I paused, thinking that Edward would open it. He just looked at me for a moment and then proceeded to walk right through it. Of course, I thought. We can just appear wherever we want to go, and it should have been obvious to me that we can walk through objects. I was still very green in the ways of ghosting.

He then proceeded to walk through the farther perimeter fence which, I assumed, had been erected by the security company. Outside was an overgrown track. Even though I couldn't fully feel the fresh spring breeze, my memories of the physical, living body were still recent enough for me to appreciate it. I started to manifest myself to accept touch. I wanted to feel the cool breeze for a moment and the sun's warmth. Edward suddenly looked alarmed.

"Begging yer pardon Miss Angela, but you don't wanna do that. Someone may see you."

"But there is no one about is there, Edward? Surely we could sense them, wouldn't we?"

"Not if they had one of those there telescups, or bino thingies," he replied, "then theys could sees you from afar. You don't wanna be attracting attention Miss, you never knows who might be awatching from afar!"

"Oh! you are so right Edward, and I have so much yet to learn."

"Also, you have to think about the energy, Miss. If you are a-manifesting then that takes a might more energy than just wafting about. On a warm day like today, that is no problem. There is loads of energy around you can pick up today. But on another day Miss, you might wander too far and it may get cold-like. Then, if you been manifesting yourself solid-like, you might not have enuff energy to get you home agin. Then you has to wait Miss, till there is enuff energy for you to 'sorb!'"

"Oh, you are so wise, Edward. I am truly lucky to have someone like you to guide me," I truthfully told him. Edward manifested a blush at this compliment. Looking shyly down at the ground he led the way towards a path which headed into the woods.

"So, what would happen if I lose energy, out in the woods on my own Edward? Should I be worried about anything in the woods?"

"No Miss, er, Angela, you will get energy back again. Never heard of any one particular ghost who never got their energy back, Miss. Just you may have to wait a while. I mean there is always energy about. Through the creatures, through the ground even, more out here than in the houses Miss. Arthur reckons that the reason a lot of modern people have lost touch with nature is that they are ins'lated, in their modern houses. They no longer touch the earth with their bare feet. They miss out on the energy from nature and therefore, nature no longer communicates so well with them. They have then forgot, and they needless destroy nature, finking it is their enemy, when it is really their friend, see? He says that he now sees that a lot of illness is really down to not connecting with nature no more. As well as people making themselves feel guilt over what is really nothing, Miss. Just you's only knows it's nuffing when you's dead like us, Miss."

"I think I understand that Edward. I believe that more people are beginning to understand the damage we are causing to the world. This damage is making the world unhealthy. I must admit that being outside I feel more sensations, in a way, without being able to touch anything."

"That is because you are picking up on the energy, Miss."

"If that is so, why do we generally stick to the house Edward? Wouldn't it be better to wander about the woods like this?"

"It's 'cause nature can be too much sometimes, Miss. Arthur can explain it better than I can. But sometimes you have too much sense of nature and you become overwhelmed. Also, like you nearly became vis'ble, Miss that can happen too. Then people come looking for you and you have to move. You'll understand more soon, Miss. But best to stay safe in the house. Also, some like Arthur become attached to m'mentos! Arthur likes his things. He has things in the loft which belonged to him. He says that they still have some of his energy Miss and he likes to enjoy it before it becomes just atoms."

"So what happens if I am trapped sometime out here and can't get back?"

"Then them times you use the trees, or the rocks, or whatever you can find."

"Trees or rocks, how?"

"I am gonna show you Miss," Edward said proudly. "Arthur asked me to show you 'cause I spend more time wandering out here than any ghost about, Miss." Edward seemed to puff with pride at the thought of his mission.

"Just two things you must remember Miss," Edward went on, "rocks is for quiet time and trees is for loud time."

"Quiet time and loud time? I don't think I follow."

"Don't worry, Miss. I'll show you – then you'll know. Trees is what the witches use to see the world, and rocks is where you can be quiet."

"Witches?" I asked. "Surely they are people from fairy tales? They can't possibly exist, Edward. Surely not?"

"Oh, they do, Miss. But, I said too much. Becomes too confusing for yer. Arthur never asked me to s'plain about witches – best you forget what I just told you and ask Arthur later."

I thought about this. It was just another leap of faith to believe that in all the wondrous revelations I had come across since my passing that there was still lots more to learn. It seemed a daunting task. What if I kept on finding newer levels of information, until I couldn't take any more? Until it all crowded in on me and I discovered that I wasn't up to my task – whatever that might be. Would I become mad? Would I be judged insane and sent two steps back to being a creature again? I felt slightly despondent at the enormity of things.

"Where are we going, Edward? Are you taking me to Tilly, are we trying to find her?

"No, not yet, Miss. First, I gotta take you to the old lady, the tree. She is a Beech and is not far now. Been here for years – since before me. I remember playing on her when I was alive. She is the best one for you to find out about loud time. She will show you gently like, for your first time. And she will tell the others that you are of good intentions, Miss."

"The old lady? That sounds intriguing. Lead on Mac Duff!" I said.

"Oh, my name is not Mac Duff Miss, it was Crane Miss, Edward Crane."

"I wasn't making fun Edward. Just misquoting, Shakespeare, that is what I was doing. And what should I call the old lady Beech tree, has she a name?"

"Oh. Shakespeare – I heard of him before Miss, when I was 'live. No – she ain't got no name. No trees have got a name – they don't use names – they don't need to. They just know who they are and who every other tree and plant is. They just knows it."

"Right, another concept I need to get my head around."

"That's Okay Miss, we'll be there in a minute and then you'll understand."

Edward led on for a couple of hundred yards, over gnarled tree roots, mud and puddles which the sun hadn't yet been able to reach and dry out. Along a winding path through the woods. In a short while we came to a clearing, in which stood a magnificent, huge, Beech tree!"

"Here she is, Miss," he gestured with his right arm and made as if to introduce me to a member of a royal court.

"I just got to ask her permission first, Miss."

With this, he touched the tree and stood with his eyes closed in silence for about a minute.

I almost felt that he had fallen asleep with his arm supporting him against the huge bole of the tree, when he suddenly seemed to awake as if coming out of a trance. He let out a gasp as if he had been holding his breath under water for a long time and just managed to get up for air in time.

"She says it's OK Miss. She is ready for you," he said taking a step backward.

I hesitated and looked at him. I was unsure what was expected of me to do, and also a little afraid.

"What am I to do?" I asked uncertainly.

"Just as I did, Miss. Touch the tree, and shut off all your other senses. The tree should accept you and draw you in. Then you'll understand, and then you'll know, Miss. Don't be scared. Remember, I was afraid of you once, Tilly called me 'Scaredy Cat', do you remember? And now I know you aren't to hurt me, Miss, and I trust you. Trust me, and trust the old lady tree." He spoke with such calm that I believed him and instantly felt reassured.

I leaned forward and touched the tree. And then I knew. The whole world opened. And I felt myself drawn into the tree, and as I did, I connected. I connected with nature, I connected with the planet. I instantly felt a rush as if the whole world was present at the same moment. I could sense anywhere, people, places, plants, suddenly swimming through the oceans, then back on land, exploring mountains, flying with the birds in the air and out over cliff tops. The tree, without talking, welcomed me, it directed me, showed me how to navigate. Out through the roots, energy flowing, energy flowing out, through other roots and back again. It was like a thousand fairground rides at once. Something as small as seeing a couple of dog walkers on the outskirts of the wood we were in, and their two dogs; a jogger the other end of the woods; a bird watcher in a hide in a bush. To other extremes of sensing the toxic waste of chemicals poisoning trees and animals everywhere, even on the other side of the planet. I instantly knew that everything was connected. Everything was part of the same. The tree, calmed me, helped me to focus on areas I wanted to explore. Even so, the experience was almost overwhelming and I needed to get out. Get back. The tree understood and gently released me outside.

I gasped. I was back outside, touching the tree. I let my hand fall down and stared into Edward's face. He had a massive idiotic grin on his face. His whole demeanour was like a giant question mark.

"Well?" he asked. "Do you understand now, Miss?"

I slowly nodded, still in wonderment, still in shock. Still not sure if I had absorbed the enormity of what I had just experienced.

"Right," he said, "Let's go and find Tilly now." I silently nodded and started to follow him along another path. A path I knew to be the right one.

After a moment he asked me. "You know where Tilly is, don't you?"

"Yes, she is playing by the brook at the end of this path." And then I thought – I have never been on this path – how do I know this?

As if reading these thoughts Edward said, "You know because the tree showed you. You know the whole of the woods now. Just takes a bit of time to get used to using the trees. But you'll learn." He carried on walking. I followed as if dazed.

Tilly was expectant of our arrival. She had sensed us approaching. "Hello Mama, hello Edward," she called out just before we left the trees to the clear embankment side.

Tilly was playing by the brook as I envisaged. A couple of water voles were scuttling around quite close to her. As we walked up, they just carried on with what they were doing and didn't take a blind bit of notice of us. I was amazed, for a second time that day. Then I realised that we weren't living people. To them we were no threat at all. They weren't actually ignorant of the fact that we were there, they just didn't care, because we never affected or threatened them.

"Hi darling," I called back. "How are you?"

"Fine Mama, just playing."

"As always," smiled Edward.

"Eddy, did you show Mama the trees?"

"Yes, Miss tried the old lady out."

"Oh, did you like it, was it fun, Mama?" she asked.

"It was unbelievable," I replied, still trying to comprehend the enormity of what had happened.

"You like it then. You also come out of the trees with a lot more energy than you went in." She faced Edward. "Did you show Mama how to do the same with the rocks. Edward?"

"Not yet," answered Edward.

"Is it the same with the rocks, Edward?" I asked.

"No, the trees is loud... the rocks, the rocks is only quiet," he said. I noticed that he had started to lose his stutter when talking to me and I was pleased that he had begun to trust me more. Now I just had to cure him from constantly addressing me as 'Miss'. But that would come in time.

"We'll do the rocks another day, maybe tomorrow," he said. "But if you are ever out alone and you need to hide, or get more energy, you can always go to the trees. The rocks is mostly about hiding and questions. But they don't have much energy."

He then turned away from me and started to play with Tilly whilst I sat by the brook in the sunshine. I had a lot to think about on this beautiful spring day.

Chapter 7

On Witches, Rocks and Leprechauns

The next day Arthur came into the living room shortly after I had arrived there.

"Good morning, Angela," he politely greeted me. "I heard you took a trip outside yesterday."

"Yes, it was lovely. Edward took me and showed me the tree. It was quite amazing. Exhilarating even!"

"Yes, it is, isn't it? Didn't have time to do the rocks though?"

"No, I think Edward felt that I had had enough excitement for one day and wanted to ease me into things."

"Wise lad, that Edward, I did tell him not to push too much onto you. He was the best one to show you, though, as the fields and what is out there is his speciality. He is a real child of nature."

"Arthur, can I ask you something?"

"Yes, of course dear, what is it?"

"Arthur, Edward said something about witches. Maybe he was just confused over something he'd read but he said that I should ask you."

"Right, right..what exactly did he tell you?" he asked pensively.

"Oh, nothing much. Just that they use the trees to see the world. Do they really exist, Arthur? Witches and all of that?"

"Well they do sort of, my girl," he said.

"What, women who fly on broomsticks and hold Masses in the woods where they sacrifice chickens and run naked around campfires, is that all true?" I asked half-mockingly.

"Sort of, again, Lass," he said.

"Well bits and pieces of that used to happen in certain countries though maybe not all the same for all witches. They seem to vary somewhat. And, they are not always women. Though women do seem to be the majority."

"Can you tell me more?" I asked, half suspecting that this was an elaborate joke being played on me by Arthur and Edward. That Edward would jump out of a cupboard and they would both roll around laughing at how foolish and gullible I really was. Was this pay-back because the 'drawing the curtains' joke had fallen a little flat, I wondered? But no, I couldn't believe that Edward would be put up to such a thing.

"Well, you remember when I first started to instruct you in the ways of souls and the living? How souls can waft around but can't manipulate the physical world in the ways that a living person can?" I nodded. "Well, witches are living people, but they have a few of the same higher senses that us ghosts have. They can see and sense more than the others living. It doesn't mean that they don't die, get hurt or feel any less than a living person does. But their heightened sensitivity helps them to manipulate the physical world in a way that other living people can't. This is their 'Magic', so to speak. Some say that they are the descendants of ancient druids. In other cultures they would be the shamans or witch doctors. They have a strong connection to nature. Hence Edward must have thought to mention them in relation to the trees. Witches use the trees as we do. Though they aren't able to enter the trees in the same way that we can. Sometimes witches also call upon us to help them."

"Do we have to do what they say?" I asked.

"Good Lord, no, girl. Witches are only human at the end of the day. As such, they don't always make the correct choices. Sometimes their egos can get the better of their decision-making, and so you have to take care deciding whether to help or work with them."

"How would I know what is the right thing to do?"

"Well, you have passed over, and see the bigger picture. The general rule is that when what they want to achieve, coincides with your goal, then that is the time to work with them."

"And how would I know that, Arthur?" I asked, puzzled.

"When your instinct tells you so. Then you will know. But don't be afraid that they will easily mislead you. They can influence the living and manipulate them with hypnotism and potions and what-not. To get them to do their bidding etc. But the dead are not so easily led astray. You have seen what is on the other side, and so in a more powerful position than them."

After a thoughtful pause, he said, "But I wouldn't worry about any of that, my girl. The last witch to live in these parts passed over herself in the 1970's sometime. I haven't seen one for years – so it is unlikely you will be bothered by them."

At that point Edward entered the room.

"Begging your pardon, Miss Angela, and begging your pardon Mr. Arthur, sir, but I thought that today would be a good day to show Miss Angela all about rocks."

"Yes, Edward, quite right you are," said Arthur. "I have a few things I need to be getting on with myself, so along you two run."

I doubted that Arthur actually had a to-do list of urgent jobs about the place. If he had, then maintenance of the property must have been far down on that list. However, I respected the fact that he made Edward feel important in his tasks – as if they took priority over Arthur's own. All the self-confidence that Edward could get would help him feel better about himself. This was all for the good. I mused on the fact that in life, people like Edward, who have the best intentions for everyone and everything about them, are normally the ones who are pushed down, without a say, whilst the louder, less worthy push themselves forward. I remembered the words, 'And the meek shall inherit the Earth'. Maybe, just maybe, this is why we had come back as ghosts? Were we the meek, now being allowed to stay on the Earth for eternity? No, that couldn't be the reason why we had been chosen to come back.

I let Edward lead me outside as we said our goodbyes to Arthur. When outside I mentioned to him that I had asked Arthur about 'witches'.

"Oh Miss, he wasn't annoyed, was he, that I had mentioned them? I didn't mean to, it just came out like!"

"No, don't worry about that Edward. Arthur wasn't angry at all. He just explained to me a bit more about witches and their ways."

"So you understand everyfing now, Miss?"

"I am not quite sure I understand everything, Edward, but I learnt a lot more."

"So I can talk about them now and Arthur won't think I am being too pushy, Miss?"

"No, I believe that Arthur will be fine with it all."

"It was Arthur, it was he that said that if I had lived longer then I may have become a witch. He said it was because I understood nature. When I crossed, I had a flash of other lives I lived and I think some I was like a witch in them. So I finks he is rite!" Edward excitedly blurted out.

"Really? So like I said yesterday, Edward, I am in the best possible hands to be shown around outside."

Edward blushed and looked down at the ground. But I could tell that he was pleased. After a few moments he asked me,

"You know where the word 'witch' comes from do you, Miss? I love learning all about words, and where they come from. Arthur has a book in the loft about that, about words which come from past people like the Celts, Unglow-suxons, Vikings and Romans and such. He shewed me once."

"No. I assume from the word 'wicken', does it?"

"Well, yes, but they both come from the same place, Miss. Do you know what that is?" He acted as though he wanted to impart some great secret.

"No, where does it come from, Edward?"

"It comes from the word 'Why' – 'Wi' of Witch being short for Why, Miss. It is because the ancient ones wanted to know 'why?' They were the first seekers of Wisdom. This is before, people, they believed that religions was the answer. Afore they all lived in houses, with heavy shoes on and no longer connected to the ground and nature and things, and afore they thought they knew all the answers through their science. Before they woz so 'Wi-se', Miss. It, nearly everything, is all about the question 'Why?' and words like 'Wizards', Miss Angela."

I was astounded at this revelation from Edward. I had never even considered this as an option whenever I had heard the term witchcraft.

"And this was in the book that Arthur showed you, Edward?" I asked.

"No, no, Miss. I know it because, I knowed it. I have always known it. And the trees, well they told me I was right."

Then I believed it was true. Because Edward was true and the trees were the wisest living things on the planet. I also wondered if this was why the church had persecuted witches over the centuries. Was it some sort of eternal battle for monopoly, over the understanding and distribution of wisdom?

As he walked ahead, taking almost the same route as before, but this time turning early to head to the brook, Edward spoke. "When you're in the rock you are safe, Miss. You can hide in a tree, but you can be found in a tree. When you hide in a rock, no one knows where you are until you comes out again. Rocks are a great place to hide as someone can only find that you're in there if they try to enter too. So it has to be a ghost, or a witch to find you. Witches can only go in through their minds, but us ghosts – we can go all in. The rock only lets one in at a time. So ifs you tries to get in a rock and it won't lets you, then that's likely coz there's someone in there already. A ghost I mean. Just think that if you was on a beach, like Cromer, Miss, there's millions of rocks and pebbles. No one would ever find you then if you didn't want them to. They'd have to try every rock and pebble there and they would most-like give up with a big headache, Miss."

"Mm..I remember seeing a few people staggering around Cromer with headaches. But mostly they looked like they had just come out of a pub or two," I said.

Edward grinned at this remark.

"What you need to think of is a question that you really want to ask when you are in the rock, Miss. You don't always have to ask a question, but if you go in the first time then it is best to ask one, just so's you know how they work."

"What, like where I left my car keys?"

"No, Miss. If you lost something then it would be better to ask the trees. They don't always have the answer as the thing you lost might be somewhere they can't reach. Like up on a shelf somewheres. No, it has to be a bigger question. A "Why-like", question. But be careful, not to ask it too much as sometimes it can take ages for a long, long answer. You don't want to be in there forever, Miss."

"So you mean a philosophical-type question? Will I have to actually have to go into the rock, like I did with the tree?"

"Yes Miss, philli-sop-holy sort of question, like you say, is fine. But like I say, not too big a question that it takes ages. And yes – you will go into the rock, Miss."

"It'll have to be a big rock, Edward, and I can't remember too many of them in Norfolk. Not like the Yorkshire Dales, or the West Country. They have huge rocks there."

"It could be the tiniest pebble, Miss. You'd be surprised how big they is inside. They is massive, so they are."

We came to the brook and Edward asked me to wait whilst he found some rocks, pebbles or stones. "So I need more than one, do I? Must be because I am such a large girl," I joked.

Edward replied seriously, "No Miss, you only need one, but you gotta choose! You think about the question you gonna ask." With that he leapt down the embankment of the brook and started searching for stones. He found 5 of various sizes and used energy to levitate them in a row on the ground, in front of me. "Here they is, Miss, you have to choose one. Do you know your question yet?"

I started to say, "I think I am gonna ask either why bad things happen to..." He immediately, put his hand out to my lips, "No Miss. Best you don't say it to me out loud. Keep it to yourself until you are in there. And don't do no 'either', either. Just one question, choose just one. Right, make up your mind and pick a rock."

"OK Edward, I think that I have made my mind up about the question. What happens next. Do I touch the rock and 'whoosh' I am confronted by a jolly green leprechaun who grants me a wish?"

Edward looked startled, "Oh please Miss, dunna ask me about Lepricorns. Ol' Arthur'd be mighty angry if he'd knew I told you about them!"

I arched back and stared at him stunned, "What, leprechauns are real?" It seemed a million thoughts entered my head at once as I wondered when the miracles would cease. Would I be totally mad by the time they ended?

After a couple of minutes, Edward began to laugh. "No, so sorry Miss. That was just a joke! There ain't really no leprechauns as such."

I exploded in laughter and we rolled about the bank of the brook for a few minutes.

Edward said, "You, wait 'til I tell Tilly, she'll laugh, so she will." And we laughed again, imagining Tilly's infectious laughter.

"You really got me that time, Edward. Much better than Arthur's curtain joke, but please don't tell him, as that might upset him."

"Well Miss, if he would get upset at that, you'd know what I'd say to him?"

Still chuckling I asked, "No Edward, what would you say to that?"

"Well, I would've drawed meself up like me Pa did, jus' afore he would make a speech. And I would say to Arthur, 'Well Man, like them there damned curtains, you should PULL YOURSELF TOGETHER MAN!' That's what I would say to him, so I would."

We rolled around laughing for about another few minutes after this. Just imagining Arthur's face and Tilly's laugh when we told her. If we had been real enough to cry real tears we would've cried ourselves dry. In the end we stopped and Edward said, "Now Miss, if you picked your question, now is the time to choose your rock. It is the voice inside your own head – may seem different – but it's that will put into words the answer to your question. No jolly green Lepricorn, Miss." We both smiled again.

"OK, Edward, I have my question." I looked at the 5 stones to rocks in front of me. They were still wet from the brook, and so glistened a bit in the sunlight. A small dingy brown pebble, a yellowish one next to that, a blue – almost Turquoise - one next, followed by a dark jet black one and the largest of them all, a big flint-stone.

"Eni Mini, Miny Mo, I choose that one," I said, pointing to the blue stone. "What'll I do next?" I asked.

"Just think of the question, don't say it, just fink it! Touch the stone and imagine you are inside, all the while thinking of the question."

I did what Edward had told me and all of a sudden I was in a massive void. A huge, dark, silent chasm, which wasn't hollow, but I could move through it. It was cool and very, very quiet. I almost forgot the question and then started thinking of it. Putting my whole concentration into it:

"Why do some people, those who seem to have everything, still have huge tragedies in their lives?"

I pictured all of the rich and famous people I could remember from the television or newspapers, who, on the face of it, seemed to have everything. Celebrity status, money to buy anything they wished for, the choices to go where they wanted. And yet, despite all their advantages, bad things happened to them on a huge scale. Suicides, drug addiction, loss of a child etc. I thought about this for a while. I felt I had been there for a decade almost when the answer started to appear in my thoughts and seemed to be voiced by some mystical woman, though I knew it wasn't a voice. It was in my own head and the voice came from a part of me.

It said, "In terms of what you understand. It is Karma! Karma, - success comes with a price."

I knew I wasn't meant to but I asked a second question, "So success, in life, is punished?"

"No, you do not fully understand," said the voice. "When people feel they don't deserve success, either because, they have stolen it from someone else, or because they have sacrificed things of value to get it, then, after a while they feel guilt. The guilt attracts negative energies, the guilt may also attract demons. These negative energies or demons play on the mind to torment their victims. This then leads to bad things happening. Guilt and self-incrimination bring their own self-inflicted punishment. Some, a few, however, never have any form of guilt for any of their actions. These people are the most dangerous even after death. Beware the one you call Devlin."

Suddenly I felt a massive coldness, and a dark, pitch-black presence. I looked forward into a shape which was appearing before me and which looked back at me. Stared ice cold into my soul. And I knew that to be 'Devlin'. He was of a darkness so dense he nearly drew me into him, my energy was going towards him. He pointed a long bony finger at me and screamed in a rasping voice, "Witch." I was petrified.

I was back outside the stone. The warm sun was still up, but I felt that it was just before sunset. I felt sensations akin to shivers. I was pleased that Edward was there still and felt safe with him close by. We had to get back to the house.

"Are you alright, Miss?" asked a worried Edward. He could see the panic on my face.

I sat up properly, and said, "Yes, let's get back now please, Edward."

"Yes, Miss. The energy level has dropped and it will be dark soon. Best we head home."

Later that evening I spoke to Arthur about what had happened and he seemed concerned. "It was just an image you saw of him, Lass. It wouldn't have been him. When you are in rocks you are safe. You are alone."

"But how would I see an image of him when I have never ever seen him before? Surely that image had to come from me? I am sure that the rock didn't conjure it up."

"Well, you might have seen him before, Angela," he said, still looking slightly worried.

"When? I am sure that I would have remembered."

"He was around when you passed. I didn't want to say anything before, because it is you alone who have to come to terms with your passing."

"Arthur, please tell me. Was Devlin responsible for my death? I just can't remember it. My thoughts seem to skip over anything around that time. It is like I was sedated and I can only remember leaving a friend's house, getting into my car and driving. I can't remember past that point."

"I cannot tell you any more at this stage, my girl. But don't let your fear of Devlin get the better of you. Fear is for the living – not for the dead."

Chapter 8

The Artist and the Lovers

Tilly came to get me the next day. I had sort of made the blue bedroom my own. "He is coming," she said excitedly, "my friend, Josh. Please, come and meet him, he will be downstairs soon."

"Oh, I am not sure that I should, Tilly. Maybe, you and Edward being there is enough, my dearest? Maybe three, with me, would be a crowd, isn't that too much?" I must admit that even though Josh sounded nice on all accounts, I was still afraid of the living.

"Oh, please Mama. I want you to meet him. He was my special friend and it would mean a lot for me if you came when he was here."

"OK, my dear. Give me a bit of time. After he has been here a while and you are all settled, I will pop my head in and you can show him to me. Is that OK?"

"Please Mama, come. There is nothing to be afraid of. Josh is warm and friendly."

I was still a bit afraid and Tilly could sense this. However, I told her that I would definitely come down when they were all settled.

I heard the creaking of the back door, and some footsteps across the flagstones of the kitchen. I assumed that was Josh entering. Although I no longer possessed a heartbeat, I did feel the nervous energy fluctuating throughout the house. I was amazed at how nervous I was. To have a living person in the house felt a bit like an intrusion into your safe space. I suppose it is the same sort of feelings which come over living people when they feel that their house may be burgled. Or maybe, if they felt that they were being haunted by ghosts?

There were some more noises, some movement of furniture, some rustling, things being set up. Then there was quiet. A peaceful quiet. The living creatures of the house got back to spinning their webs, scuttling through the dust and dirt. The moths and flies, flittered around, reflecting sunlight streaming in through windows. They flew between tasks and trapped themselves in webs. I felt more at ease.

After putting it off for as long as I felt I could, I sensed where Tilly and Edward were sitting and carefully transported myself next to them. Tilly looked up and smiled at me. She was lying on her front, face forward, elbows on the ground and her head cupped in her hands. Josh had his back to us and was facing the window, lightly sketching with a pencil into a sketch pad. Edward just sat on the floor, legs to his side, totally absorbed in what was going on. I felt an energy from Josh which was easy to absorb. It was a light energy and ever so calming. I suddenly understood what was meant by the absorption of energy, as described by Arthur. After a short while I also began to feel at ease in Josh's presence.

Josh was a tall thin lad. I had thought that he would be a bit more like my former boyfriend, for some reason. But whereas my boyfriend had looked healthy and strong, more muscular, Josh seemed frail and almost effeminate. Almost like you would imagine a poet of the romantic era being. He had a pale complexion too, like he had been unwell. I supposed that a lot of his demeanour was due to the trauma and grief he had suffered from losing a mother at such a young age. I felt sorry for him. But I was also pleased in the knowledge that he was channelling his energy into something constructive such as art. As an alternative, grief could have very easily led him to spend his time on self-destructive habits such as drinking to excess, or drugs. It was no wonder that art was used by many as a therapy.

His drawings were very good. Better than I could do, and, although I don't like to say, probably a bit better than my boyfriend had done. Though I don't think that my boyfriend had fully developed his skills and would probably have improved since I had last seen him.

Josh was sketching for almost two hours. He was so engrossed in doing what he was doing. He had no thought for what else was going on around him. At one point, Tilly got up and walked over next to him. At first I thought that she just wanted to get a closer look at how the drawing was progressing. Then I realised that she was extremely sad. She touched him, and tried to connect with him. She touched his forearm. He stopped and brushed away at a spot on his arm as if an insect had crawled up over his bare skin. Tilly looked frustrated. She started to manifest. Taking his energy, she started to attempt to show herself to him.

Edward was instantly at her side. He tried to draw her away. "No, Tilly, that is not right, it's wrong." Tilly tried to pull away from him and carry on. "Tilly, you have to stop. This isn't the same Josh! He has growed up. You'll scare him."

"He is my Josh," said Tilly.

"No, no he's not," repeated Edward, "he is old now. Olduns' don't see like young-uns' do. He won't understand." Tilly struggled a bit in frustration, she became annoyed. Energy was abruptly released and something crashed.

Josh started and looked around. A picture had fallen from the wall and lay with its frame buckled and glass broken. Josh turned and stared at it in wonderment. Tilly seemed to awake from a trance. She let Edward bring her back over to me. I held her. This was the saddest I had seen Tilly. Edward had passed her to me as if he was at a loss what to do. I hugged her to me and stroked her hair.

Josh yawned loudly as if he was suddenly drained of energy and started to pack his things away. He got up and stretched. The sun was hidden behind clouds and it became cooler. Then, the creatures of the house changed colour. Dull greens and insipid yellows, dark browns. They felt fear. Tilly looked around.

I felt fear. "What's happening?" I asked.

"It's others," said Tilly.

"What, other people?"

"Yes, outside."

Tilly seemed to concentrate so hard whilst looking to the perimeter security fence which surrounded the house. I tried to copy what she was doing, but could only feel the presence of movement and shadows and just make out the presence of two people.

Tilly turned back and whispered, "It is those whom Arthur calls 'the lovers'."

Josh put his satchel over his shoulder and made to leave. He went back, out through the kitchen and I heard the back door shut behind him. I went to the window and watched him walk up to the security fence and along to some bushes. He bent down and disappeared through the brambles, and probably through a hole in the security fence.

A few minutes later a man, I hadn't seen before, emerged from the same bushes. A few seconds later he had turned and helped a woman through the brambles. She was wearing a short leather skirt, black, low-cut blouse and leather boots. I thought this was an odd outfit for such a trip in the countryside such as she was undertaking. But, on reflection, felt that the clothing was appropriate for what Shakespeare would have termed 'Country matters'. It was Spring, after all!

The lady was making a show of coughing and spluttering, and waving her arms about as if she was fighting off hordes of gnats. She brushed herself down and turned and addressed the man.

"I wonder who that was?" she asked.

"Don't know," the man said. "Probably some young guy come in here for a secret wank!"

"Oh, arghh," she said, with excitement in her voice, "Maybe, I should've gone in first and helped him out, eh?"

"You're a sexy girl you are, Tina," Patrick said, then, "lucky we saw him, or I don't think we would have found where the new hole in the fence was. They keep mending the damn thing!"

She reached up and kissed him. He pulled her up further with one arm and put his other hand under her skirt and started to caress her between the legs.

"Come on, let's get inside afore anyone else comes along. I am as horny as hell."

They held hands and he hurriedly pulled her towards the house and in through the kitchen and into the living-room. "Do you think that he was doing it in here?" she asked, "I can't smell nothing. Young lad like that – must have a strong smell of the sea."

I was surprised that I didn't feel waves of disgust at the way she talked. In life, as the other Angela, I would have. But now, it didn't really bother me. I was detached from the prejudice of life's conformities. And this talk seemed of such little importance now.

"Probably, upstairs on the bed we use," he said. "He probably smelt the fish from you and had a wank there, thinking about you."

"Oh, I hope so," she said excitedly.

"Come on, or I'm going burst outta me pants," he said and holding her arm dragged her upstairs to one of the smaller bedrooms. It was the bedroom that Arthur told me that they liked to use, and I had made preparations.

As they walked in Patrick suddenly stepped back a pace.

"What's wrong?" Tina asked.

"Someone's been in this room," he cautiously replied.

"What do you mean, Pat?" she asked.

"Look, this here screen wasn't here before!" he replied.

No, it wasn't I thought. It had taken a couple of hours for me and lots of combined energy, with Edward's help, to levitate and lift the heavy thing from the cellar, where it had probably been for about 50 years, and get it set up in this room. I was determined that if Tilly and Edward were going to be absorbing energy from these shenanigans then they would do it from behind an Edwardian dressing screen.

As we had been moving the screen Edward had told me, "This used to belong to Mrs. Partridge who lived here before, when I was here, Miss Angela. I remember it. She used to be so proud of this screen. Mr. Partridge had it shipped up from London on a wherry to Coltishall. Then they brought it here on the cart."

I was interested in this piece of history and encouraged Edward to carry on talking. "So that must have been about 1905 then?"

"Yes, Miss, or maybe later – '08. I passed in 1910. Seem to remember – 'bout just after the King died. He was an Edward too, Miss!"

"Oh, him, I remember, they said that he used to stop off in Gunton on his way back from Sandringham and meet up with Lily Langtry there, didn't he?"

"I remember he went there, Miss, 'cause I remember being roped in to beat for some of the pheasant shoots, Miss. But I wouldn't know whom he met there. I just was remembering about this screen though. Mrs. Partridge, you know what she used to use it for?"

"Undressing behind, Edward?"

"Yes Miss, but she had it mostly in the parlour. She used to have afternoon tea, when the men folk was in the fields working and the ladies used to come 'round. Well, they would sit around, talk about fashions and then they would try on each other's clothes and sometimes, some of 'em would bring in other clothes for them to try."

"How did you know about that Edward? Surely *you* were working in the fields?" I'd given him a sly look.

"Well Miss, Annie, the maid, told me about it, Miss. Then, the men, one day they says, 'We forgot one of the shovels. Best we send young Edward back for it.' And me Miss, I was keen to help so I says 'Yep I'll go'. But something was amiss 'cause them fellows was all grinning right across their faces. Well I come back Miss, but had forgot 'bout the 'Tea Party'. As I crossed the back garden I just peeked at the parlour window and there was Miss Ward, the 'prentice from the drapery. She was standing there at the window in just her pantaloons and nothing else, Miss. I was flabbergasted, Miss, but you know what Miss?"

"What Edward?"

"She just smiled at me, winked, and blew me a kiss, Miss."

"What did you do, Edward?"

"Well, I just ran Miss, fast as I could. In the shed I didna remember what shovel I'd been sent to get and so grabbed the three I found and carried them faster than lightning back to the fields."

"The men – they didna need to ask what happened, Miss, as my face was red and if I had fallen on the floor, you would've mistaken me for a beetroot Miss! They laufed and laufed Miss. So's they did."

I laughed a little as I felt that Edward now found it more amusing than the trauma he had thought when it first happened.

Edward, smiled too. "You know, Miss – for three days after that you could have roasted potatoes on my face alone, Miss!"

"Seems like Miss Ward had a bit of a soft spot for you, Edward?"

"I think so maybe Miss. Not 'cause of that so much, but I saw me own funeral, Miss. And I was in the churchyard, and Miss Ward was there and she was a-crying and crying. And no one could console her for days after. I always wonder, Miss, if I dinnae pass like, well even though she was about 2 years older than me, maybe Miss eh!?"

"I know, Edward. I think we all have something like that we wonder about," I replied. I felt a strange connection to Edward's recollection as I had been two years older than my lover.

Patrick took a move towards the screen. "Best have a look around it. Don't want no 'idden camera filming us at it do we?"

"Speak for yourself, Pat. I'd like to do a porno. My 'usband would love to watch that."

"Still can't get me 'ead 'round that. 'Ow your ol' man likes the thought of us 'aving it off!" he said.

"He's just a randy cuckold, gets turned on by it. He is probably at work at the moment thinking about it. Probably keeps 'aving to go to the loo to feel 'imself-up," she laughed.

Each to their own I thought.

Patrick had a good look around the screen, just to make sure that there wasn't anyone hiding there. I even looked around to see if anybody was there, and then realised that I was, but neither of them could see me. I had sort of lost my fear of the two of them when I realised how pathetic and comedic they appeared to be. I had begun to control my fear of the 'living'. Maybe the longer I was a ghost, the more I would lose the prejudices of life and become less judgemental.

Patrick returned to Tina and had pushed her back down on the bed, kissing and caressing her. She started to undo the buttons on his shirt. Behind the screen I could see what was going on through the lattice work, especially where it had decayed and been eaten by insects over the years. Arthur materialised next to me.

"You haven't run for the hills then, but have decided to stay and watch?" he asked me.

"No, I am more curious now. I am actually learning a lot about human nature here," I replied.

"Mm, study – is that your excuse?" he asked, chiding me.

Patrick suddenly stopped his seduction of Tina and sniffed the air. "What's a matter?" she asked.

"Can you smell pipe smoke?" he asked her, whilst looking around the room.

"Not going on about that pipe smoke again are you? It's your 'magination, it's just these ol' houses, they stink. Come on – get on with it afore I lose the urge."

"They don't just stink, they're filthy as well," he replied.

"And don't I just love a bit of filth. And this bed, someone could 'ave died in it. That really turns me on, that does."

Arthur leaned close to me and whispered, "If I lived a 1,000 years I don't think that I would have ever gotten turned on by someone dying of cancer."

"Me neither," I whispered back. Not that they could hear us though.

The next hour or so they went at it like two automobiles at a stock car rally. Arthur was right, they gave off a tremendous amount of energy. Both Tilly and Edward came in and hung around behind the screen picking up some of that energy.

Half an hour into it and Edward said to me, "And that is why I call you 'Miss', Miss!"

I was puzzled again and so asked him what he meant.

"Well Miss, this screen-thing, it is sumfing loike my teacher would've thought of, Miss," he said with a big grin across his face.

"Don't be too cheeky now my boy," I answered, "otherwise, I will have to get Headmaster, Mr. Arthur, here, to give you six-of-the-best with his old cane."

We laughed and Arthur looked as if we had both been impertinent and gruffed through his pipe.

During this time Tina and Patrick, the lovers were getting their clothes back on. Tina was saying, "You gave me a lovely bruise there, my 'usband will be pleased. With the scratches I got from going through the brambles earlier 'e'll think we had a great shag. Give me a right spanking he will!"

"Still don't properly understand how your marriage works," Patrick said.

"This affair quite saved our marriage," said Tina. "Things were getting really boring before that and we were only staying together for the sake of the kids. This has put a spark back in the both of us. If it weren't for this I think that we'd be divorced now. I can put up with a lot of things, Pat, but boredom is not one of them. I crave excitement. Otherwise, what have you got in life? Nothing, it's just one long stretch of hard labour!"

"Me and Viv' are alright," said Patrick. "We're happy enough most of the time. Just, she is often too tired when she gets 'ome from work to do anything. Mostly sits on the sofa and snacks watching dramas on TV. Just likes a bit of a cuddle and falls asleep. Put on a bit of weight, so she has, these last few years. We could do with an 'oliday. That'd put the spring back in our step."

"A holiday don't always change things. Maybe whilst you are away, but when you are back to the grindstone, things soon slip back to boring, ol' normality. Sometimes you got to make the decision to change things completely like me and Tom did. Otherwise, you gotta move on and start again. What may seem a strange relationship to others, our debauched life-style, well, I think the same about them. They just have their heads down and trot along until they pop their clogs. Never happy. No idea they is even alive. Some can't even stand the sight of each other. Who's right, them or me? I am happy in doing what I am doing, Pat. And if you find it too strange, I can always find someone else to have illicit sex with and you can jog-on back to ol' Viv' and fall asleep on the couch!"

"Hold on. Tina, I didn't say anything about finishing us! I am just saying I wish that Viv' didn't have to work such long shifts at the Care Home. She is always so knackered when she gets home. That's all. Something will happen to get us back to how we were."

"Nothing 'appens lest you make it, Pat! Until then, life's as boring as shit! And as 'they' say, 'You can't polish a turd'!"

"Maybe, you're right Tina. Maybe, all this ain't really hurting anyone. We're just having some fun and excitement after all."

Tina was pulling her boots back on. "Maybe we could up the stakes?" she asked.

"Up the stakes, how? I thought this was kinky enough as it was?" answered Patrick.

"What if we got another person involved?"

"What a three-some? You know of some lady or bloke who'd be up for it do you? Best be careful though, the more people involved the more chance that things may get back to Viv'. And I ain't quite ready to get into that sort of excitement just at the moment."

"No – no one in particular. But I just had a thought, what if – we came here a little earlier next week and that young guy was here? What if I came in alone whilst he was 'aving a wank and I sort-of 'elped 'im out a bit?"

Tilly immediately stood up and looked angry.

"What will I do then, just leave you both to it and go for a walk?" Patrick sounded disappointed.

"No, you could sneak 'round back and watch through the window."

"You're making me 'orny again. Fancy a quickie, one for the road?"

"Doesn't have to be just imagination, Pat. We could do it for real, next week."

Before anybody had a chance to stop her, Tilly had walked through the screen, and started to materialise. Edward went after her and tried to calm her down and get her to come back.

Tina shivered. "Wow, it has just turned chilly in here," she stated. The room seemed to darken over as if the sun had gone behind a cloud. "Probably best we get back now," she told Patrick. She stood up and started adjusting her clothes in the wardrobe mirror. And then, suddenly, screamed.

Patrick jumped up. "What the hell?" he asked.

Tina was pointing at the mirror. "I ju, just saw a little girl standing behind me looking at me in the mirror." she stammered, trembling. Patrick looked in the mirror and then around behind Tina. She stood shaking, looking straight ahead, as if she was afraid to turn around.

"Is there anything... is it still there?"

"Nahw, ain't nothing there, must have been a shadow when that cloud just passed the window," he said.

"I could've sworn I seen her," Tina insisted, "a little girl with a sour looking expression on her face, staring straight at me, she was."

"Like you said, Tina, life's a tad boring without a bit of excitement eh?" said Pat as if he was doubting whether or not Tina was making it up for dramatic effect. Then jocularly, "If you don't want another shag you can just say so, you don't have to start making excuses, babe!"

"I saw something," Tina snapped back angrily, "come on, let's go."

Edward had managed to get Tilly back behind the screen. She gripped hard on to one of my legs, not sobbing or sad but in a determined stance of anger. I stroked her hair, trying to soothe her.

Shortly after that she powered down. She drifted up into what I had started to consider my blue room. It was nice and dark in there, easy to relax in. I turned to Arthur,

"I am a bit worried about Tilly, Arthur. What if this woman tries to seduce Josh?"

"I know," he answered. "I have never seen her like this. But she must understand that we can't meddle in these affairs. It is for people to make their own choices in life. It wouldn't be the first time a young innocent lad was corrupted by an older woman. It seems to be part of the course of life, the journey from innocence to corruption. It is what makes us what we become. As we grow older we all make mistakes, we all have choices in life, they become our experience, our history. They become our final 'US'."

"You sound like you talk from experience, Arthur?"

"Oh, I do, my dear. I was no saint in life. In 1916, I was an officer in the Army as a recently qualified doctor. At the frontline in France. Baptism of fire, so to speak. I met a young French lass and we had a fling. Nicole was her name, nurse, beautiful long dark hair, when she let it down, and jet-black eyes."

"That sounds innocent enough," I said.

"Well, it would have been. But I was already married to Irene."

"Oh!" I said feeling that he was honestly opening his heart to me.

"What with how things were going out there, we dinnae think that we would live through the next day. It was hard to believe that we would ever see Blighty again. Home became a distant memory very quickly out there you know?" he lamented. "Still, no excuse really. I was a married man and forever, felt guilty afterwards. Found it hard to look Reeney in the eye when I got back. Every time I touched her I felt a wave of guilt come over me. Reeney though, thought that I was suffering from the effects of the war. She had seen others who'd come back a lot more shell-shocked than I was. She was really gentle with me. In a way that made it a lot worse."

"That was the past," I said. "They were different times then. Extreme times, you shouldn't have felt guilty."

"In a way, I know that now. But when you are living these things seem really important. That guilt led me to go downhill for a bit. Stayed out a lot, in the pubs, drank far too much. Then one day I thought, 'This has to stop' and I told her, told Reeney. It broke her heart. I wished afterwards that I had had the courage to keep the secret. Seeing her pain made it a thousand times worse. But she stuck by me, and in the end, we made it work."

"All ancient history now," I said to reassure him.

"Maybe. But do you know what the worse part was, aside from Reeney's pain?"

"No what?"

"The worse part was that even though I loved Reeney, and she was the Mother of our children, the worse part was that I was, 'in love' with Nicole. And I felt so much pain and grief, and anguish over that."

"I am so sorry, Arthur," I put my hand on his arm and he manifested acceptance of my touch.

"Always wondered what could have been. What should I have done? Couldn't leave my wife and young kids to go swanning off to France! Had to stay put and man-up. I got a letter from her about a year later. She had sent it via a British nurse who had served there with us and was a mutual friend. In it, she pleaded with me to return and see her."

"And you didn't go?"

"No. Kept the letter for about a year. In the end walked off into the woods by the old lady Beech tree, with a bottle of whisky. After one last read of the letter, I burnt it. And almost drank myself dead. Woke up around 3am with my back against the tree and staggered back here. Tried never to think of it again."

"As people, as the living, we really do hurt ourselves when we love, don't we? Eh, Arthur?" I reminisced about my own experience and my own broken heart.

"Aye, Lass, I suppose we do. These here pair of lovers may be a bit off track but at least they are getting a bit of fun whilst alive and don't waste pointless time feeling guilty about it. Who knows, maybe they are doing the right thing eh? At least they are enjoying themselves."

"Well, she certainly is, anyhow. I am not sure that I can say the same thing of him. He doesn't seem 100% onboard," I replied.

The two had completely dressed now.

Tina said, "Come on Pat. Let's get outta here. Place seems more creepy than seedy now," and made their way out the back and on, through the hole in the fence.

"You're right about another thing, Arthur."

"What's that, Lass?"

"I now have loads more energy. It's like a caffeine overdose. I'll probably be up half the night haunting the place and bouncing off the walls."

"If you want my advice, my girl, read a good book. Lots of them in the loft, you know."

And with that we both left the room.

⌁⟨⟩⌁

Chapter 9

The Paranormal Investigators

It was that weekend they came for the first time since I had been in situ at the house. Since being a ghost. The Paranormal Investigators, or 'Ghost Busters' as I liked to call them. I heard the movement but had been so engrossed in a book that I hadn't noticed their arrival. Maybe I was losing my fear of the living? Edward came and told me that they were here.

"Is there anything I need to do Edward?" I asked.

"Not really, Miss. Arthur normally advises to just keep out o' their way and let 'em get on with it. He says that they will find the ghosts that they have made up in their own minds to find which 'e says will probably be greatly helped by our house rat scuttling about and a touch of the wind. And that will be that."

"Well it isn't that windy today, so I can't see that having much of an effect, Edward."

"Arthur reckons they bring their own wind with them Miss. Both from their yapping, and out the 'tuther-end, if you get what I mean, Miss?"

I smiled at that and nodded.

He continued, "They'll set up at the moment and pop back when it's dark. Some of the extra energy is good though, Miss. Probably not the other-end wind-energy. And Arthur'll probably be up to chat with you about them soon. They seldom come up in the loft, Miss. Think that they're 'fraid of going through the ceiling. So's if you's wanna stay here and read, Miss, should be fine."

"Where's Tilly?" I asked slightly worried over her last encounter with visitors from outside.

"She's down by the brook. Playing most-like. Don't worry about her, she don't have no interest in them. But she will know they're here already, most loike!"

"And what will you be doing, Edward?"

"Me Miss? I might have a nose about. Sort of follow them. The girl Jane, who comes with the two fellows, well I like her. She seems to have a bit more of a sense for things than the two fellows. F'some reason, I feel a sort of connection to her, Miss."

"Is she pretty, Edward?" I asked, wondering if he had a crush on her.

"No, it's not that, Miss. I mean, yes, she is pretty. But somehow I feel like she is related in some way."

"Like another cousin, Edward?"

"Sort of, but not 'xactly. Bit hard to es'plain, Miss."

"Alright Edward, I don't understand exactly, but I trust your senses. See you later. Have fun."

"Bye, Miss."

"Bye Edward, see you later."

I tried to carry on reading my book but my imagination got the better of me as I heard clumping around downstairs and indistinct chatter. I decided that at some point I would have to have a peek at what was going on. Just at that moment I smelt the familiar pipe-smoke fill the air around me and Arthur appeared.

"Hello my dear, you've heard that we have guests, I think?"

"Yes, Arthur, Edward popped up and explained to me."

"Thinking of having a peep, were you?"

"How did you know? Sometimes I believe that you can read my mind, Arthur."

"Call it the experience of a wise old ghost," he said. "It is just in our nature as ghosts to be curious, I believe. Especially when we aren't a 100% sure of why we're here and what our mission might be. As much as we dislike the interferences of the living, we can't help but wonder if their presence may have something to do with our destiny as ghosts."

"Yes, I can see that," I said. "Edward seems to think that he has a connection with the girl ghost buster. So maybe he thinks that she has something to do with his reason for being here, do you think?"

"Might be. But I think that it may be because she has the potential to become a witch."

"A witch? Did you mention that to Edward?"

"No Lass, as I am not a hundred percent certain, but she does seem to have the instincts of one. That is why Edward can sense a link. They are both children of nature and potential witches. Or, rather, Edward had the potential, once, but this young lass has the qualifications to go forward and become one."

"How would that work?" I asked, "Is it dependant on her turning a corner one day, taking a slightly different fork in the road and 'Hey Presto', she can suddenly weave spells and turn people into frogs?"

"No, not quite," he said thoughtfully, puffing away on his pipe. "No, what she would need really is a mentor. Someone who knows the ropes, so to speak."

"Strange that she should seek out ghost hunting as a hobby eh, Arthur? As if she is searching for something, but doesn't know that what she really needs is someone to take her under their wing."

"That is, if she is what we think she may be. Lots of potential witches never, ever become full witches. I suppose that a lot of potential surgeons are out and about cleaning windows, sweeping roads or playing the bassoon in a jazz band somewhere, because life never gave them the breaks to get what they needed for the next stage in their journey to become a surgeon. Born to alcoholic parents, or not having the references to get into the right educational establishment. Unfortunately, a lot of what you become is down to who you know, rather than what you know, even now, still!"

"Nature versus nurture you mean?"

"That's what they call it now, is it? Almost sounds like you have a choice in a woolly environment with soft edges. Unfortunately, there are a lot of sharp edges out there in the real world."

"Do you think it is safe for Edward to follow her about then? I mean, if she has heightened senses then she may detect him."

"Edward knows what he's doing. Let's see what pans out. I trust Edward to not be seen when he doesn't want to be. He has been doing this a lot longer than either of us. Remember how shy he was about meeting you at first?"

"Yes, I remember. He stayed away from me for weeks, but I could sense him sometimes."

"Well, this young girl can sense him all she wants, but seeing him is another matter. Edward will be three steps ahead of them all."

"Would it be such a bad thing if we communicated with them, Arthur? Surely it would do no harm and they would feel that they have achieved something in life. Wouldn't that be a good thing?"

"Is it a good thing? Lord no, Lass!" Arthur looked aghast. "Could you imagine if they saw us, let alone caught us on a camera? All hell would let loose. They wouldn't just feel content and say, 'Oh, well, that's that then', and move onto something else in life. No, my girl, you know as well as I do that if the world gets a whiff of happenings from beyond the divide then the whole world would go bonkers. See what happens at them Catholic shrines, for instance. Some young girl gets home a bit late because she has dallied with a young lad from the village. She decides to tell her parents a porky-pie along the lines of, 'sorry about being home a bit late Pater and Mater, but on the way home the Virgin Mary descended from the rock above the village pond'. Next thing you know, people are selling the water bottled, and jumping in the damned pond to cure their piles. No Lass, we can't have that here. How long, if they caught one of us on camera, or proved our existence, how long before the whole house has been dismantled and people up and down the country have our bricks sitting on their mantelpiece as souvenirs? No, we definitely can't have that my girl, we'd be out on our ear. And for what? Just so some jumped-up sprog can sell his 'Ghost Hunting Biography', and go off to America to do spiritualist lectures? No – I should coco. What good would there be in it for anybody? Also, if people didn't fear death any more, they would be jumping in front of trams willy-nilly in the hope that the next life they would all be born millionaires. Can't have that, Lass!" Finally Arthur seemed to run out of steam and his rant ended.

"OK, OK, I get it," I said in desperation, exhausted from listening.

"But, like you said to me once before, there may come a point where a method of communication between the dead and the living would be useful."

"Quite, but that time hasn't come yet, my girl!"

Suddenly we noticed that the noise downstairs had ceased and everything was deadly quiet. I looked at Arthur.

"Looks like they've set their equipment up and popped off for some nosh. They'll be back after dark," he said.

I gave him a cheeky look and said, "Bagsy, I am first one to play with their kit whilst they're away," and with that I disappeared downstairs, leaving a perplexed Arthur to call after me, "Be careful, Lass, there are cameras which are geared to go-off when triggered!" And he hurriedly came after me.

Downstairs looked the same as before and at first I was a bit disappointed. Then I noticed a light blinking off to one side. Arthur appeared before me, crouched and whispered as if we might be overheard. "Careful, Lass, the whole place is booby-trapped, worse than the Hun could do!"

I had a vision of him crawling through 'no-man's land' between trenches in his uniform, respirator attached and flapping at his side, pistol in one hand and a knife in other to cut trip wires. Whatever you thought of Arthur's opinion about smacking, or the youth of today, he was a hero nonetheless. Our haunted-house-hero till today.

We both sensed the movement behind us at the same time and turned. It was Edward. "It's alright," he said, "I know where the cameras and thingies are set up."

He then proceeded to show us where the various gadgets were, and explain a bit about them. "This by the door plays a tune if anything passes over the invisible wire. It is sensitive to movement and also supposed to be sensitive to energy. I walked past it though and it didn't go off! Then there is three cameras. One at the bottom of the stairs, one in the kitchen and one in the parlour. They, too is sensitive to movement. Our kitchen rat just had 'is portrait done. His family should appreciate that. Picture comes out the bottom of this one 'ere."

"That's a Polaroid camera. I used to have one. Clever how they've rigged it up though!" I said. "The other one over there, by the bottom of the stairs, well that's a cine camera."

"Always thought I would make a good movie star myself," said Arthur, "I'd make a good Cary Grant!"

"More Charlie Chaplin, sometimes," I joked. Edward grinned too, but Arthur gave us both a hard stare for a couple of seconds.

"I don't know what this is," said Edward pointing to the fireplace. "Looks like a messy spider's web to me, made by a spider that has given up on life. There's another one on the staircase."

"Oh, that. That's a dream catcher," I said. Then went on to explain. "I had a friend who brought one back from holiday in America. She had bought it at an authentic Indian Reservation. These two here, look more like Great Yarmouth gift-shop! Can't see what good they would do though."

"Oh, Miss, I like the thought of genuine Red Indians turning up. We once had Buffalo Bill's Wild West Show come to Norwich. I didn't get a chance to see it but they had beautiful posters put up in Coltishall and Walsham. So bright and colourful, those posters. I looked at them for ages and imagined I was in the West. Also, Illustrated News run articles on it and there were some exciting pictures of Cowboys and Indians and a lady who could shoot a

Winchester at a target when she had a scarf covering her eyes. Do you think a real Indian ghost would be summoned tonight?"

Arthur interjected with a cynical sneer to his voice, "I very much doubt it, me lad," and gruffed into his pipe.

"Me neither," I added. "These don't look like they could catch a cold, let alone a dream or two of an Indigenous Native American!" They both gave me a blank stare. Edward said,

"I was talking about Indians, Miss. Real fierce, proud, Red Indians, Miss. Not Indiginies er, whatever else you just said Miss." He looked disappointedly at me as if I didn't understand.

"Yes, that's what I meant Edward. My mistake," I reassured him.

"There is also this whirly thingy here on the sideboard. Not sure what that is," pointed out Edward.

"That's a tape recorder, oh, and it's running. I do hope that they haven't picked up our conversation," I said.

"No, Lass," said Arthur, "it would be pretty difficult for you to manifest a voice so that the living can hear. I mean, we feel that we are chatting to each other with our voices most of the time. But in reality, it is more like telepathic thought. Makes sense really. We don't have voice boxes any more, so how would we make sound? It requires a lot of energy to produce sound, like the energy Tilly released the other day at that Tina woman. You gotta be pretty angry. Then the sound comes from your energy and whatever is to hand to transmit the vibrations you give out. Pretty hard to do that in a coherent manner, let me tell you. We only feel like we are talking to each other because that is what we were used to in life."

"Oh, OK then," I said thinking about it. "It's a pity really. I like a good old chin wag!"

"That's a good old expression," he said approvingly.

"My mum used to say it," I replied. For a moment I was lost in thought of home and the past.

"If you wanna talk to someone, Miss, someone living that is, go to the trees!" Edward stated profoundly.

"What, you have to go in the trees and then you talk to someone through that?" I asked curiously.

"No, Miss. You could only do that if yous woz to talk to a witch. No Miss, the trees – in summer - you makes the leaves rustle and it can whisper voices. The leaves, together, they can vibrate the voice. Takes a little practice, but I done it afore. I talked to Miss Ward and told her I was OK and she had to live her life the best she could. That made her happy, that did. And it don't hurt the trees none too."

"Well, that is interesting to know," I said

"I'll show you sometime, Miss," said Edward.

Arthur held his pipe away from his face and said, "Well even I have learnt something new today."

Just at that moment Tilly came in through the veranda doors. "Hello, Granpa, Hello Mama and Edward."

We all greeted her.

"What's happening?" she asked.

Edward rhetorically answered, "Well you know those Ghost hunter people are here. Well we're looking at their gadgets and toys and what-nots! Miss Angela woz just 'splaining what some does – or s'posed to do rather."

"That's boring" she said. "I just like it when they walk around asking them silly questions. They look funny don't they Ed?"

"Yeah they do, Tilly. But what woz also 'cxiting was that your Mama, sorry Miss Angela, was just talking about red Injuns what she calls native indigenius or some such thingy."

"That is exciting, I like to play Injuns." With that she started holding her hand over her mouth and whooping and hollering like she was doing a rain dance. Edward started laughing and joined in too. Within minutes they were a cowboy (Edward) shooting his six-gun at the injun (Tilly) and then suddenly something in their antics, and energy release, triggered about 3 of the devices. Flashes went off all over followed by the sound of musical chimes. They immediately stopped dancing and looked frightened.

"Bugger, that's torn it!" swore Arthur.

"Have we done something wrong Gran'pa?" asked Tilly.

"No, you're alright, my girl. Doubt if them cameras caught anything of significance. I think that maybe the house-rat will take the blame for this one. Especially as he was caught on camera earlier."

The rest of us laughed with the release of tension.

Just then Tilly stopped and looked around.

"They're coming back," she said.

Tilly's sense of what was happening at a distance seemed far greater than the rest of us as it was a few moments before we all picked up on the motion outside. When they were near the perimeter fence,

"Action stations," called Arthur. The other two stood to attention. I felt a bit left out and asked Arthur, "Where do I go to, Sir?"

"Tut, tut, one shouldn't talk when not spoken to in a situation like this, my girl. Await further instructions." He looked severe.

"Sorry, Sir," I shouted.

He smiled and said, "Just kidding with you, my girl. You have permission to go wherever you wish."

"I'll follow Edward," I said, thinking that this would be a safe bet.

"OK, young Tilly, looks like you're with me, my little girl," he told her.

"Aye Sir," she replied to Arthur, saluting so that her hand covered her whole face. I felt like picking her up and giving her a big hug. She looked so cute in her smock dress and purple velvet jacket. Then I wondered if she would think less of me because I had chosen to go with Edward and not her. But she did look happy to be with Grandpa that I thought I must have been needlessly worrying. After all, it was just a game we were playing, wasn't it?

I didn't know why, at that time, but the three 'Paranormal Seekers' actually came around the front door and spent a few minutes trying to get that to open. It did eventually give, but was a bit warped with damp and held fast by ivy creepers, so that it took a few moments to creak it ajar enough to squeeze inside. Earlier they had used the back kitchen door when setting the equipment up. So, this puzzled me. After all, that was the wisest entrance point. The one that most people used when coming in here. Later, I realised why they had done this. For dramatic effect. The two lads were being filmed by Jane on a cine-camera. I remembered my dad had had one, similar, when we had our holidays on our boat on the Norfolk Broads and, also, at Overstrand, by the sea. So the entrance, through the main door had been a show for cinematic effect. What more did they have in store for us, I wondered?

The largest lad, a young man in his late twenties, I later found out to be called 'Mitch', was talking into the camera as if he was David Attenborough exploring the darkest African Jungle.

"So fellow Paranormal Seekers," he was saying. "Here we are again in this haunted North Norfolk house. We've been here before, but it has such a presence, such an aura about it that we have to keep coming back, until it opens its deep, darkest secrets to us! I can't give you any specific details. We need to respect the previous occupants and protect the location. But I will say that the locals have reported strange ghostly, goings-on at this place. Lights on in windows at night, when no living soul is about, and no electricity present. A woman in white is said to glide across the fields and wail, with outstretched arms, as if seeking her long-lost, dead lover." I looked at Edward at this point. I was wondering if there were such a legend. He looked back at me and, as if knowing what I was asking, and shook his head.

He voiced, "Never, ever been no white lady 'ere, Miss. There's supposedly one over at Worsted, but not 'ere Miss!"

As Mitch walked forward he started describing, to the camera Jane held, the hallway as if it were different from a thousand other hallways, "Hat stand, still with a couple of hats, all cobwebbed over. Couple of walking sticks and an old umbrella still sitting, as if waiting for their owner to pick them up and go about the day's business. Just waiting, awaiting the return of their dead owner. Oh, My Giddy Aunt, just look at the old wooden, staircase. All this intricate, hand-carved detail."

I looked at it wondering what he was talking about. Even with my limited knowledge of carpentry and fixtures and fittings, I could tell that the stairs were made to standard specifications and fitted together. The patterns and spindles were machine-turned.

"Hey, Keith."

"What, mate?"

"Do you reckon this staircase is medieval? I feel it is giving off medieval vibes, Mate!"

"I reckon so, Mate," answered Keith.

Arthur gruffed in his pipe. "No, they're not, them stairs and bannisters are 1920's. Harry Paterson, the carpenter from Hoveton made them. I had them fitted myself to replace the old ones! All the rage at the time so they were."

Mitch stood back and admired them. "Yeah, definitely medieval, mate." He looked back into the camera, Jane was holding. "Countless ghosts have probably travelled up and down these stairs since the time of Elizabeth I. Who knows if anybody had been pushed down, possibly by a disgruntled servant or mad monk, even?"

As a group of ghosts we hadn't split up into our groups yet and were still together. "Complete idiots," said Arthur, "the house is old, but it's not that old."

"Hopefully, we'll catch some of the spirits of the past residents on film tonight as we explore this ancient haunted house," carried on Mitch.

"Mitch, Mitch, come quick," Keith called from the next room.

"What is it Keith?" called back Mitch.

"Mate, you won't believe it, mate, but all the devices have been tripped. We got ghosts, mate!"

"Oh, darn!" said Arthur.

Mitch stared back into the camera. "Well, fellow psychic investigators, it looks like we already have proof of paranormal activity. Just shows that all our hard work has paid off. Follow me as we find evidence of those spirits forced to walk the earth in penance of past misdeeds."

"Miss-deeds?" asked a baffled "Edward, I don't think I have done any miss-deeds! 'Ceptin that time we scrumped some apples from the orchard at Howes farm. Don't think they would send me back all this time for that, does thee?"

"No, Edward, I think you can be forgiven for that," I said.

He looked at me with a big grin and said, "Well, that be a weight off my mind, Miss!" We both laughed.

We followed as Mitch went into the next room, huffing with anticipation.

"What's been triggered?"

"Well, about all of it. Looks like the music box has gone off, a couple of the sensors. And the three cameras have flashed."

"Quick, check the Polaroid."

Keith quickly walked over and looked at the Polaroid camera. "We've gotten something!" he shouted excitedly. He took the ejected photo which was still hanging on the bottom of the camera. He looked at it and shrieked.

"What is it mate?"

"Mate, you are not going to believe this – we've got a demon, mate!"

"Demon, mate?"

Mitch snatched the photo from Keith and looked at it. He shrieked and threw it on the floor, jumping backwards against the wall in fright.

Jane focused the camera on the photo lying on the floor. She leaned down and picked it up and looked at it. "Hey, guys," she said laughing, "I don't think we've got a demon. I think that we've got a rat!"

"Rat?" asked Mitch angrily. He snatched the photo from Jane's hand and stared at it. "Oh!" he said. "But, you can easily see why we thought it was a demon. With the flash and all, and being so close to the camera, it looks like a demon."

"Definitely, looks like a demon to me, mate!" Keith reassured Mitch.

We all laughed hard, me, Arthur, Tilly and Edward.

"Bloody pissy rat. If I get my hands on it I'll wring its bloody neck, so I will," said Mitch.

Edward stopped us laughing. "Stop, stop, she is looking, she can see us."

We immediately stopped laughing. Jane was staring hard straight at us.

Arthur said, "I don't think she can see us. But she can sense something and she is not sure what." I felt a shiver. The thought of the living seeing the dead was creepy.

"I am gonna have to set everything up again guys," said Keith, "bloody pissy rat." He used Mitch's words.

"We'll have to edit that film as well," said Mitch. "Nothing of interest for the viewers to see there."

"Have you got the car keys?" asked Jane. "I'll go back and get another film cartridge from the car."

Mitch handed Jane the keys and she left. Edward told us that he was going too, to make sure she got there safely. I thought how off it was that neither of the boys offered to escort Jane back through the fence and along the track to where the car was. Instead, they let her go in the dark, alone. Luckily she had Edward with her. She couldn't be in safer hands.

Mitch spoke to Keith, "We're gonna have to get someone else to do our filming I think. Jane doesn't get it. I could have sworn she was laughing at us just now. When she came for the job, she said that she had an instinct for the sort of things we do, but she don't seem to understand."

"You're right, Mitch, she's a bit of a know-it-all if you ask me. Don't see why you took her on. We were fine on our own."

I looked at Keith a bit more closely and wondered if his adoration for Mitch was based upon something a bit deeper.

"Well, it'll be her loss when we sack her. I know she doesn't get any money from us, but look at the opportunity she has with the wealth of ghost-hunting knowledge we've got. Just think of all the years of experience, between us Keith."

"Yes, mate, you're the most knowledgeable person I know on the supernatural, so you are," said Keith, glowing with admiration. I looked at Keith again and thought, 'Yes I am sure I am right'.

"Mitch, mate?"

"Yes Keith?"

"Can I ask you something, mate?"

"Sure mate! What is it?"

"Well with this investigating and all, I was thinking that your name – well Mitch – it's a good name, and well you're in charge mate, so it is good that you have a cool name an' all!"

"Thanks, mate."

"That's alright, mate. But what I was thinking that my name, 'Keith', well I thought that I could have a different name to 'up' my status a bit. Never really liked that name and it don't sound too adventurous."

"A different name? But you're already 2nd in command, mate! That's a good status."

"2nd in command, Oh, wow, mate, I didn't think you saw me as that."

"Yes mate, you always been 2nd in command, mate."

"Wow, if that's the truth, can I have a new name to go with it – something which would give me a mysterious, sort of paranormal investigator image?"

"What name was you thinking of, mate?"

"Well I thought instead of Keith it could be 'K', mate!"

"Kay? That's a girl's name innit mate?"

"No – the letter 'K'. I could be rebranded as 'K'."

"Yeah.. whatever you want, mate! If that's what you want I will henceforth christen you 'K'."

"Oh. Thanks mate, you don't know how much that means to me. I could eventually become known as "The Dark 'K'." Mysterious eh?"

"Hang on, mate I ain't calling you that!" Mitch said, slightly alarmed.

"Why is that, mate – too much, you think?"

"Oh mate, with your dad being Jamaican, people would think I was being a racialist mate. I can't have my public thinking that."

"You ain't no racist Mitch, I know that. We always been mates from school. I known you forever and you never been racist." Then after he had thought, he added, "Oh, OK mate, we'll just stick to 'K' for now!"

"'Kay' it is then," agreed Mitch looking a bit suspiciously at Keith.

After a while Jane came back from the car. Edward came back over to us. The 'Paranormal Seekers' started their filming again. They actually took themselves outside once more and started as if it was the first time of entering through that door. This was even less convincing than the first run. Strangely, Jane wasn't sacked on-the-spot. I supposed the lads had nobody to replace her at this late stage. Somehow though, I doubted that they would get rid of her as long as she carried on doing the job for free. All mouth and no trousers – as my Mum would've said about them.

Nothing out of the ordinary, if you could call these two comedians ordinary, happened for a while. They moved from room to room with an electronic gadget, held by Mitch which looked a bit like a Geiger Counter. An arrow flashed on a scale, backwards and forwards, at certain points. Mitch declared that some parts of the house had more spirits than others. I just felt that it was detecting his heart-rate more than anything and at times when it was blinking a red light, we, the real ghosts, were nowhere near him or the device.

Arthur had hung back downstairs a bit and I went to see what he was doing alone. He was in the parlour looking at some of their equipment which they had placed on the sideboard. "What are you up to, Arthur?" He was deep in concentration.

"Sssh!" he replied and then I realised that he was levitating something, a small packet, from one of the bags. He lost concentration and the thing he was levitating fell.

"Damn," he said. Then the packet bounced across the sideboard and dropped down the back.

"That'll do," he said and seemed pleased with himself.

"Have you just stolen something, Arthur?" I asked, frowning.

"Nothing they will miss, my dear," he said.

"What, what have you taken?"

"All will become apparent in time, my dear. All in good time."

"Well that isn't a good example for the children," I said.

"What, 'the children'? 'The children' who are older than the both of us put together?" he teasingly asked.

"Well, wonders will never cease. Stealing is something I would have never expected from you of all people, Arthur!"

"You will thank me for this one, my dear."

I looked curiously at his sly demeanour and asked him why.

"All in good time, my dear, all in good time," he repeated.

"OK, I am going back to join Edward upstairs and follow their progress. Where's Tilly?" I asked.

"Oh, she got bored and went to play with the house rat in the kitchen," he said.

"Remind me," I said indignantly, "that if I ever have kids in my next life, never to hire you for babysitting."

I chastised him further. "Just imagine coming home from a good night-out, to find your kids playing with rats!"

He gave me a whimsical look.

"OK, off I am, back with Edward," I said. He waved me away and the next instant, I was beside Edward as he watched Mitch and Jane walking around one of the many bedrooms.

Edward filled me in, "They have just started to ask the questions, Miss."

"Questions?" I asked.

"Yes, Miss – it is what they do – they ask their ghosts the questions, Miss."

"Shouldn't they be asking us?"

"Well, in a way they do think they is asking us, Miss. And they would be asking us if their questions was sensible, Miss. But most times they ask dumb questions, Miss!"

"Like what?"

"Just listen to them, Miss. You can make up your own mind if they is 'telligent or not."

Mitch began intonating in a hollow call, "Hello, are you able to speak to us? Can you channel the energy? Connect with us?" Nothing but silence.

"Are you sad? Was your passing premature? What is your name? How many are you? Is the white woman here who is said to haunt the place? Do you want us to be here? One knock for 'Yes', two knocks for 'No'," Mitch asked in quick succession. Even I was confused which question he wanted answered first and doubted that any bright, experienced, ghost would be able to answer, with clarity, all questions in a logical sequence.

"We mean you no harm. We are just here to communicate. We are here to help you if you are trapped here. Here, inside this house. We will help you pass over."

'How the hell could they do that?' I thought. Do they have some sort of secret book with all of our missions contained in there? 'Do they know when we have to pass completely? Obviously not. Edward was right, I concluded, what they were saying was dumb!'

"If any of the spirits, here, want to come towards any of the devices we have, make the lights flicker, sing a tune, or just speak into our tape-recorder, please do not feel afraid. We are here to help you."

'Help? Help how?' I thought. 'You are just here for your own ego!'

"Look, I understand that you are unsure. I know that you will be hesitant. But I need to know. Are the previous owners of the house here at the moment?"

Mitch looked around. I looked around. As if anyone was going to answer this question.

Edward said, "He is clutching at straws there, Miss! They is abroad. Gone to live in South Africa, Arthur told us."

That's interesting I thought, will have to ask Arthur more sometime.

"Is there any one here who died, unexpectedly?"

I paused and thought.

"Was anyone murdered in this house?" he asked.

Edward suddenly shot a worried glance at me.

I stopped suddenly as if someone had pierced my chest with a huge blade.

"Murdered?"

And then I realised. Me, it was me! I had been MURDERED!

I released a wave of energy. A few doors slammed shut and a vase fell off a chest of drawers and smashed to the ground in the room. Two of the windows simultaneously flew open.

Almost immediately, Arthur appeared beside me. "All right my dear, alright, you are. Easy now. Take it nice and slowly," he said, reassuringly.

And it started to come back to me. Not the whole circumstances, but also the realisation that I had been murdered. Killed before my time. My body lying on the ground, naked, broken and beaten. But why, how, who would...?

Keith shouted, "Oh, mate!"

"Wow!" shouted Mitch. And then, almost threateningly, to Jane, "Just tell me you caught that on film?"

Jane nodded. She was staring at me hard and looked nonplussed.

As soon as I saw her expression and felt her stare going through me I calmed down.

"But how? Why was I killed?" I asked Arthur.

As Jane continued to stare I indicated her to Arthur and asked, "Can she see me now?"

"I am not certain, but I think that she may have gotten a glimpse of you when you released the energy."

Then I thought of my naked body I had seen lying on the floor as I had passed over. I made my arms cover my body and asked Arthur, "Can you see me? Am I naked?" I felt shock and hurt rising in me all at once. Had I been walking around nude? In front of the children? I felt instant shame.

"No girl, no – you're not naked. You are in a beautiful summer dress. That is how we all see you. It must be from one of your happiest memories. That is how we all see you. Good Lord, girl. I passed by a heart attack whilst on the loo. You don't see me walking around with my kegs about my ankles and my John Thomas waving about, do you girl?"

This reassured me. Only Arthur could reassure me like this. I laughed albeit nervously.

"Well that is a vision I will have to live with now. I could have done without that one, Arthur," I said.

"That's the spirit, girl," he told me. "Chin up, think clearly. You have broken through the fog of your passing. The rest, the details will come in due course when you are ready."

"What about this? What about the release of energy? They have it on film, don't they?"

"Yes, that is a problem, my girl. Now every dam ghost-buster all over the country will be coming here. We won't get a moment's peace."

Edward spoke up.

"Don't worry," he said. "I'll soon sort that one out!" We both looked at him hard and wondered what he meant.

Mitch and Keith were excited. "That's the best response ever, mate!" shouted Mitch.

Keith replied, "Mate, just think of all the money we're gonna make from the 'merch', the vids we'll sell."

"Videos, my arse, I think this could get us on Telly mate. This is the big-time we're talking about here. We've finally arrived!"

We left the 'Paranormal Investigators' to their celebrations. Edward stayed behind, but Arthur led me away to the quiet of the blue room. After an hour or so, the house was silent. The investigators had packed up and left.

Chapter 10

The Calm before the Storm

The next day we found out what Arthur had stolen.

"Batteries, my gal!" he boasted proudly.

"Whatever, do you need batteries for?" I had asked baffled.

"Give me a few moments then you can gather Tilly, Edward and yourself and join me in the conservatory. All will be revealed."

"What are you going to reveal, when?"

"Give me about 30 minutes then you can all join me," he said, tapping his nose to show it was a secret. A surprise.

Half an hour later, I appeared in the conservatory with Tilly and Edward. It was very bright in there and although I couldn't feel it, it was probably hot too. It was a glorious day. Arthur was standing in front of a smallish, oak, country dining table. For a second or two, I thought that he must have cooked us all a meal. That would have been futile though as none of us could eat.

He stepped aside with hands out to his right and said, "Da....da!" I looked down to what he was presenting and immediately made out a small portable radio. 'But..?' I started to think, when the dial moved on it, a light came on at the front, followed by a sound of crackle. Shortly followed by Randy Crawford singing 'Rainy, Night in Georgia'. I jumped for joy and clapped my hands together and said excitedly,

"I love that song, adore it. I danced to this song the first night I met my boyfriend at a discotheque in Norwich. Oh, Arthur, you clever old thief, you."

He beamed back at us.

The other two were really excited as well and jumped to sit on the chairs around the table.

Over the next few hours we had what was the closest to a party that ghosts could have. We caught up on all of the news and listened to lots and lots more music, changing channels occasionally to seek out a genre we hadn't heard for years. The music and sunshine gave us immense energy.

I suggested a game where each of us were to say what we thought the most positive thing about being dead was. Then we would all vote, and the one with the most votes would win. Arthur started by saying that he was pleased that he didn't have to get someone to cut his toe nails any more. He then started to describe the issues he had with his toe nails since an infection he had caught in the trenches which wouldn't shift. He explained about the long, hunched nails with blackened ends which curled over. By the time he finished the three of us were staring open mouthed at him. None of us could think of anything after that, so we all voted him the winner and decided to play another game instead.

I then told them all that I had at first thought that Arthur had cooked us a meal.

"Well, that would have been pointless and silly, wouldn't it?" he replied.

"I thought so too," I said.

Edward said, "I do miss the freshly cooked bread Mrs. Partridge used to make. Cor, that was delicious, that was. Just outta the oven, butter fresh from the churn, used to melt deep into the bread. Oh, in the winter I used to be allowed to come in some times, and sit on the settle in the kitchen and get warmed by the fire. Mrs. Partridge would sometimes give me an extra cup of soup and a big chunk of that bread and I would dunk the bread in the soup. I loved that, I did. Almost worth being alive for ag'in!"

"Arthur, and I sat on that settle in the kitchen just after I arrived. Do you remember Arthur?"

"Yes, Lass!"

"I remember picturing what it would be like, people sitting in front of the warmth from the Aga!"

"Weren't that oven then, Miss. Used to be a big ol' range there, all dark from years of burning and soot, that's a newer oven that one is."

"Yes, I had that put in," Arthur almost winced as if he was to blame for taking away something Edward enjoyed.

"I loved toffee-apples. When the fair came to Coltishall, I was always bought a toffee apple," said Tilly.

"Oh, I remember toffee-apples. They were alright if you got a nice ripe apple, but the last one I had was bitter, and the toffee was so hard it broke the top off one of my teeth. Hated going to the dentist. I can still feel it even now," Arthur told us.

"Mine was delicious, always delicious," said Tilly

Edward, lost in thought, started to become more chatty, "Toffee apples makes me remember Coltishall fair. How they set up on the fields near St. James and we used to walk from there to Belaugh and back. The boatbuilders' yards and the breweries in Coltishall would have a holiday for one day. It always seemed to be sunny then. Flies hovering around ripe cows' muck which had been baked like pies in the sun. And if you was unlucky and fell on one, or likely pushed, we would all laugh. Then yous would have to go down to the river and wash yourselves down. There was always music too on fair days. Everywhere you went, music. And at night the lights from the boats all moored up, an' alls the people singing and drunken-loike."

"They had stopped those fairs when I came here to become the local GP," said Arthur. "And the breweries had mostly closed down and moved away by then. Still had boat builders – but eventually they went to Hoveton and Wroxham. Most worked on the farms, or in Mills. Then the tractor came and less were employed. Factories sprang up. Changed a bit over time it has. If you wanted a fair you had to go to North Walsham, or Norwich, or Cromer of-course!"

"Where did you come from, originally, Arthur," I asked.

"Originally, Scotland, Lass, brought up near Edinburgh. You weren't born and bred in Norfolk were you, Angela?"

"No, I was born in Guildford. My Dad moved here when I was 10. We moved to Suffield, just by Gunton, outside Walsham. He worked as a chemist there, in North Walsham. Actually, he might still work there, come to think of it."

"Did you go to school there, Walsham?"

"No – I took the bus and went to Aylsham."

"Nice village," said Arthur.

"More a town now, they keep building around it all the time. Still like a village in the centre though."

"Edward?"

"Yes, Miss?"

"Where did you stay then? You said that you used to be let in on cold nights sometimes. Surely you didn't sleep outside?"

"The small room above the stables, Miss. I used to live there."

"Good Lord, I never knew that," announced Arthur, surprised. "That is no bigger than a cupboard, that loft."

"That is sir, but I liked it, I did. That was my first real place of my own. In my house, before I became a farmhand, here, there was seven of us kids in one room. Oh, don't get me wrong, I had a good family, always jolly, but I liked to be alone. That's why I likes the woods. I like being outside. Some nights I like to go back to my room, the loft, and stay there all night. Sort of cosy it is."

"I wondered where you slipped off to sometimes," said Arthur. "And, by-the-way my boy! Where did you go to last night? And, furthermore, what did you mean when you said that you would sort things out?"

"Yes Edward, what was that all about?" I asked. Even Tilly stared at him, awaiting an answer.

"Well, you know'd when she went to the car? To get the film thingy?"

"Yes," Arthur nodded, "You were gone a fair while."

"Well I spoke to her, I did."

"You did what?" cried Arthur flabbergasted. "Do you understand what trouble you could cause? I bet she has told the other two and they'll all bring parties of ghost hunters in coaches. Especially after they watch that film from last night."

I felt nervous. 'What had Edward done?' I thought.

"No, no, it ain't like that. She ain't like that. It's hard to 'splain but she is like me. When she was walking to the car, she spoke to me first. She said, 'I know that you are following me. You can talk to me if you wish. I won't hurt you.' So I used the trees and talked to her."

"What did you say?" Arthur questioned further.

"Well, at first I told her not to be afraid, then I told her my name. Then I told her we, me and her, was a bit like the same. She then told me that she wasn't afraid and had sensed me and yous all, in the house before. I then told her it would be bad if lots more people came. But she should find me sometime and I could help her."

"Help her do what, Edward?" I asked.

"Help her – show her how to use the trees. Like I showed you, Miss!"

"Are you sure you know what you are doing, Edward?" Arthur asked.

"Yes, I knows I am right. I know I have to do this!"

"OK, lad. You have to do what you think is right."

"I thinks it is what you called my destiny, Arthur."

"Quite right lad, quite right. If it should be – it will be!" Arthur puffed on his pipe in thought.

Then I remembered. "What about the film? The others can use the film and see what happened last night, can't they?"

"No Miss, they can't!"

"Why?"

"Cause when them two lads was whooping and 'ollering, like me and Tilly did when playing Indians, and they was packing the stuff away I got her attention like."

"How?" asked a concerned Arthur.

"Well, I just orbed the mirror. Made lights dance in it, a show-like, that only she'd notice. Then when she came over to the mirror, I wrote her a message in the dust on the mirror. I said 'dump the film', and I signed it 'ed' so's she'd knowed it was me that asked. And she winked at me. Just like that time Miss Ward winked at me. Then she took the film thingy outter the projector thingy and showed it to me.

Then she gestured like this," Edward made a gesture with his right arm, "so's that I followed her to the bathroom. Then she unravelled the film outta the case and flushed it down the loo thing."

We laughed at this.

Arthur said, "Thank god the water is still connected. Did the others know?"

"No – they'd heard the flushing thing and Mitch called out and asked 'what was that?' and she said, she said..."

"Said what?" Arthur encouraged.

"She said, bit embarrassing, but here goes...," Edward emitted a blush, "well she said, 'Just me, I just had to pee!' and then that Keith, 'e starts, really loudly talking to Mitch saying, 'Mate that's disgusting, she's gotta go mate!' And all that how it is filthy in this place and she should've waited."

We all felt really relieved and started laughing at this.

"Well my boy, you did good!" Arthur said with pride and Edward's chest lifted.

"Well, I don't know about anybody else but I am about relieved as Jane pretended to be." And we all laughed again and Edward blushed some more when he realised what I had meant.

"Brave girl that," said Arthur, "she'll get in a lot of trouble when they try to watch the film and it can't be found."

"Somehow I don't think she'll be that bothered. I think she found what she has been looking for," and I looked at Edward. He glowed with pride. He had found his destiny at last and he felt confident that it was something he could handle.

"Well, another mystery solved," said Arthur. "All's we need do now is work out some other things, like how the pyramids were built and we can pretty much know everything there is to know."

"Oh, that's an easy one that is," piped up Edward.

"What, you know how the Egyptians built the pyramids my lad?" asked Arthur. "That's impressive."

"Course I do. We all knew it at school afore I left. When I was 12."

"They taught you all about the pyramids?" Arthur asked, slightly unbelieving.

"Oh, I heard this one before," said Tilly, "go on Edward, tell them how's they was built." Arthur and I looked from Tilly to Edward in anticipation.

"Well," said Edward, "lots of people believe that theys carted the rocks for miles and then lifted them on top one 'nother until they had made one. But that is almost impossible to do 'cause they is too heavy."

Righto lad," encouraged Arthur. "So how was it done then?"

"Well, what they did," continued Edward, "was they dug a massive 'normous hole in the ground like an upside-down triangle shape, see?" Arthur nodded uncertainly.

"Well, makes sense, when you thinks about it, really. Then, theys dropped the rocks, one by one, into the hole, cause doing that is easier than lifting them upwards, see? Then they just joined them together with mortar, you see?"

Arthur looked uncertain. "And..?" he asked.

"Well, all they gotta do when the mortar was set was just to flip them alls up the other way, and 'hey presto', yous have your pyramid!"

Arthur started to point uncertainly, as if he were about to make a counter argument, when both Edward and Tilly started rolling about laughing.

Tilly said, "He got you, right, didn't he Grandpa?"

I laughed too and after a few moments of gruffing into his pipe, Arthur began to laugh.

"Well, looks like the joke is well and truly on me," he said.

After a while of more listening to music, and even a bit of dancing, Edward turned seriously to me and said,

"I have to thank you, too, Miss."

"How so?" I asked.

"Well, afore you I was scared of talking to girls. 'Cepting Tilly, 'course. But you has given me the confidence I needed. If you'd never come then I wouldn't be able to talk to Jane, I don't think."

"Well thank you, Edward. That is a lovely thing to say. I am really pleased that you think that I have been of some use to you," I replied.

Arthur had overheard us and said, "Teamwork." We all looked at him, and in unison said, "Teamwork," and we laughed.

Chapter 11

Tilly's education

Arthur had been getting more pensive as the days passed. He paced about the rooms slightly more agitated than I had seen him before. I asked Edward, "What is wrong with him?"

"He is worried about Tilly." For a brief moment I thought Tilly was ill or something, (which was impossible for a ghost), until Edward explained further, "The living are generally creatures of habit. They do what is most comfortable. Tomorrow is a week since Josh was last here. I think that he will return."

"Oh, and Arthur is afraid that the seductress, Tina will try to have her wicked way with him?"

"Exactly," said Edward. "And Arthur isn't one for messing with the living. He thinks that they should be able to do what they want. He thinks that it is only right that destiny finds its own path."

"Do you agree with him, Edward?" I asked.

"Well mostly, Miss, yes. But not always. Sometimes you gotta step in and do something. I mean, what if I hadn't spoken to Jane, or asked her further to dump the film? We'd be in a pickle and no questions to that, Miss."

"But Jane is a potential witch. It is OK for a ghost to interact with a witch, isn't it?"

"Yes Miss, but by my action in asking Jane to dump the film, I affected the lives of those two other ghost-busters

Miss! Sometimes you gotta take that step and get between things and make the outcome different, Miss."

"I see what you mean, Edward. It could have been a real problem if that film had gotten out in general circulation. I can see Arthur's worry is that Tilly will upset, or scare that woman and she will bring hordes of people here? But won't Tilly respect Arthur's age and judgement on this and not interfere if he asks and explains that to her?"

"Oh, ghosts is not like people, Miss. With people the olders theys gets, the stronger their ego gets. But as they gets older their bodies become weaker, Miss. With ghosts it's different. Tilly is the strongest ghost amongst us. She has been here longer than any of us and each year she gets stronger – so she do! Though, on-the-face-of-it, Arthur is the senior, Tilly really is – though she is a child – the strongest. If she wanted to do something then there ain't nothing Arthur could do to stop her. Haven't you noticed how she senses things long before any of us?"

"Now you mention it I have noticed that, Edward."

"Well that is because she is stronger. If she wanted to manifest herself, Miss, she would do it twice as quick as Arthur could, and quicker than me even."

"I have an idea, Edward."

"What's that Miss?"

"Well, what if we asked Tilly to go with us on a trip somewhere tomorrow and just let whatever happens here, happen?"

"That's an idea, Miss. But I doubt it'll work. Tilly likes to see Josh and she knows he will most likely come."

"Yes, I suppose so," I said. "Maybe we can think of another way to help."

"We need one good idea, Miss. Like trip that Tina up so she falls down the well, Miss!"

I looked, but sensed he was joking mainly, and not seriously contemplating murder.

"Well, best we get our thinking caps on then," I said.

"I am at a loss," said Arthur when I caught up with him. "I am not sure how to get Tilly to understand how important it is that we don't interfere with the living. They must be free, to make their own paths."

I told him what Edward and I had discussed and gently put into the conversation that maybe we had to intervene sometimes. I used the examples Edward had given about getting rid of the film.

"But that was different," he said. "With this situation we have a young, innocent child in the celestial body of a very powerful ghost who has been here over a hundred years. She doesn't understand why she should let Josh make his own choices, why Tina isn't as much a threat as she sees her to be and how this sort of hanky-panky stuff is all natural. Just part of growing-up."

"And that, Arthur," I exclaimed excitedly, "is the answer to our dilemma."

"And what might that answer be exactly, my girl?"

"What you just said in a nutshell, Arthur!"

"Which is what exactly, my girl?"

"Sex-education."

"What education?" he asked flabbergasted.

"Sex-education. We all get sex education at school these days. Tilly has never had any, and because she passed away so young she never got the gist of things from gossip and experience. We just have to convince her that if anything happens between Tina and Josh, then it is just a harmless delve into that side of things."

"Mm, I see what you mean, my girl. I have a few of my old medical books in the loft – I suppose that I could sit down and go through some of the pages of those with her. I am a bit rusty mind but,..."

"Not you Arthur!" I stopped his train of thought from going in that direction. "You're not the best person to instruct Tilly!"

Arthur seemed a little put out. "Well I suppose you want to give it a go, do you? Though, as far as I can see, I am the only qualified GP around here with any medical knowledge."

"Neither, you nor me, nor anyone else," I said.

Arthur looked baffled, "Who do you propose then?"

"Tilly," I said confidently. "Tilly will educate herself."

He looked at me as if I had gone mad.

After a few moments I said, "Through the rocks."

"The rocks?"

"Yes, we prime Tilly with a question along the lines of 'why would Josh want to be alone with Tina?' and we get her to go in a rock, or stone – or pebble even, for the answer to materialise in her own mind, in a way that she will understand."

Arthur stared at me for a long, silent moment in which I was sure he thought that I had gone mad. I started to doubt my own reasoning and almost decided that my suggestion was a terrible idea.

"You know what, my girl?"

"No what, Arthur?"

"You are definitely a lot more than just a pretty face, my girl," he said proudly and slapped his own thigh, hard.

About an hour later, Tilly, I and Edward were making our way to the side of the brook. Arthur had stayed behind to, as he said, 'Hold the Fort'. I think that he wanted to avoid scuppering the whole plan though by putting his foot-in-his-mouth. Maybe, he also wanted me to be the owner of my own deviousness, and felt confident that I would get the result needed."

"Tilly?"

"Yes, Mama?"

"You trust me, don't you?"

"Yes, Mama."

"Well, could I ask you to do something for me?"

"Anything, Mama."

"Would you go into a rock and ask a question for me?"

"Of course, Mama, but why don't you want to go in and ask the question?"

"Well, Tilly. I thought that it was best the question came from you Tilly, as you have been here longer than anyone and I don't want to mess things up. I haven't the experience of you. You have been in rocks hundreds of times, haven't you?"

"Thousands, Mama. So many times, I almost forgot how many."

"That is why I believe that you wouldn't make a mistake. Which I might."

"OK, Mama, what is the question?"

"Tilly, I just wanted to know if Tina, spending some time with Josh, like she does with Patrick, well, whether that might help him, Josh I mean?"

Tilly stopped mid-pace and stared angrily up at me.

Her eyes seemed dark and her demeanour aggressive. "But I don't like that question, Mama. I don't want to ask that question. Josh is a nice boy. She can't help him!" I thought that she was going to turn away and slip back to the house. Her anger manifested power and I realised for the first time how strong she was. For a moment I was almost afraid of her.

"Well, if that is correct, and you are right, then the rock will tell you this, won't it? And I will feel so silly for having gotten you to ask it in the first place. However, if Tina could help Josh in some way, wouldn't that be good for Josh? And wouldn't you feel good for asking the question and knowing that something good will help Josh?"

"But I don't think Tina would help Josh," she said. "I think that she is evil."

"Then if that is the case Tilly, the stone should warn you and you can help him. But if you don't go in and ask, how will you know?"

After a few moments thinking about this, Tilly relaxed. "Alright, I will ask your question. But if the rock warns me – then I will be, so, so angry at Tina!" she said this last piece with menace.

"Thank you my darling," and I manifested a kiss on her forehead. I felt really guilty though to have manipulated her in such a way. But I felt that it was all for the greater good.

When we reached the bank of the brook, Edward had already levitated 5 of the choicest rocks he could find. I reminded Tilly of the question. She chose her rock – an amber pebble - and went in. We waited, and waited.

Finally, she came out. And, she had a sublime smile on her face.

Slightly concerned, from my own experience, I asked, "Are you alright, Tilly?"

"Yes, Mama," she said.

"What happened?" I asked.

"Well, the voice said that maybe Josh is a scaredy-cat like Edward was 'afore he really met you, Miss. And maybe, Tina would help him not to be scared any more. Then if Josh, say, one day got married, he would help his bride to be happy, because Tina helped him, and they would have loads of children, 'cause Tina helped him know, what was what, Mama! Also, it said that what Josh was looking for was a cuddle from his own mama who died when he was young, and that would make him feel happy, Mama, because he missed those cuddles when he was little."

"That's all good then?" I asked, feeling relieved that it had worked out fine.

"Well yes, but there was one warning, Mama!"

"Warning, what was that?" I asked worriedly.

"That this was all fine as long as Tina let Josh go. But if she tried to keep him somehow, then that would be trouble!"

I felt as if Tilly manifested a threatening demeanour – the air grew colder as the sky darkened.

"But you are OK with things now, Tilly?" I asked.

"I am alright, as long as Josh is alright, and happy, Mama!"

Mission accomplished, I thought.

Later that evening I related all of the events to Arthur in detail. "I feel so wrong in betraying her trust though. I felt I was deceiving her by getting her to change her views because I wanted a certain outcome," I lamented.

"Think of it as education," he said. And before I had a chance to say anything, he went on. "Education breaks many hearts. Think about where you first heard that Father Christmas wasn't real. At school probably! And then school slowly but surely erodes all of your trust in what your parents, or childhood stories, told you. Soon you learn that there is nothing exciting around the next corner. Just another mammoth task to complete. In the end, life seems to lose all of its magic. Is this not so?"

"Sort of," I answered, "but I don't believe everything you have said. There is still 'love' and that I am willing to believe keeps the adventure as to what you may find around the next corner, alive."

"Possibly, that is what we like to believe. But I couldn't 'love' Nicole. You and your boyfriend 'broke up' and the 'love' was lost? Maybe, we were too educated? Maybe, just maybe we had lost trust in 'love'?"

I felt sad.

"Maybe we just broke Tilly's love for Josh?" I asked. Arthur just held his pipe and stared at me.

"You know, all of this has probably just been in vain," he said.

"Why?"

"For a hundred reasons. Maybe Tina is just a fantasist and won't seek Josh out. Maybe Josh will get a job, and not turn up tomorrow to sketch. Maybe, just maybe even, a giant aeroplane will fall out of the sky and blow us all to smithereens tomorrow," he said.

"Maybe," I agreed. But I doubted it! I felt that we were set on a course which couldn't be determined by us. It had already been decided upon by a higher court!

"Did you know that Edward has met up with Jane a few times since the 'Paranormal Seekers' were last here?" asked Arthur.

"No, no I didn't," I said.

"Could you do me a big favour and ask him about it, please? I am only concerned about what could go wrong. I don't want him to think that I am trying to meddle though. It is just concern."

Hesitantly I asked, "You don't want me to spy on him, do you?" I didn't feel comfortable with this idea, no matter how much I respected Arthur.

"Gud Lawd, no girl! If you want, you don't have to tell me anything about what he tells you. But I know that he will talk to you. I am asking you to do this as I don't want to spy on him myself. If you feel that what he tells you is safe and good, and there is no reason to worry about any trouble coming his way, then just tell me all is fine. I trust your judgement fully, my girl. If there is a problem, then let me know. We have to look out for each other here."

Then I realised that Arthur was just being his old sweet self as a responsible Grandpa. I agreed to what he asked and went to find Edward.

He was in one of the out-buildings which had been a workshop next to the stable. He seemed surprised, almost startled that I had sought him out there. "What are you up to, Edward?" I asked trying not to have a judgemental tone.

"Well, Miss, I have been seeing Jane a couple of times and I am going to meet her again tomorrow and wanted to take her something."

"Arthur said that you had been seeing her." I wasn't going to lie to Edward as he may have sensed it and I didn't want to ever sour our relationship. I still felt a bit guilty about getting Tilly to go into the stone, even though I knew it had a positive outcome.

"Arthur knows then, does he? I thought that he might. Is he annoyed, Miss?"

"No, he is just concerned for you and wonders if you need any help?"

"No, I is fine Miss, I is."

"What are you taking to Jane then, a present?" Still aware that she was an attractive girl and Edward might feel more for her that he was letting on.

"Not quite a present, Miss. More something what 'ave been left for 'er."

"That sounds interesting and mysterious, Edward."

"In a ways it is, Miss, and can't say as I fully understands it. But there used to be a witch who'd lived in a cottage the other side of the woods, t'wards Worsted way. Them days the woods used to be lot bigger than they is now. Lot got chopped up and turned into farm land for Sugar Beet since."

"I remember hearing something about her. Oh, and Arthur said that the last witch from these parts passed away sometime in the 1970's. Was she that one?"

"Yes Miss. 'Er, name was Mistress Gunn. But afore she passed she give me some things to give to the next witch she said would be coming."

"And you think that is Jane?" I asked.

"Yes Miss, sure of it. But she still very green so she is. I tried her on the old lady tree and she was a bit wooden-like."

"Wooden?"

"Yes, Miss. Though trees is made of wood and they is full of energy and flowing through the world, a dead tree is wooden, Miss. It's no insult. It's just what we call it when someone can't get the energy to flow. Just like this ol' bench 'ere Miss. Wooden. But Jane'll get betterer at it, Miss, I knows she will. Just takes time is all."

"But some old things have some energy, you said so before. Like a residual energy."

"Yes, that is right, Miss. Over years of someone having a thing, Miss, that can absorb some of the person's energy. It is like it remembers certain things. If there is a tragedy, Miss, then emotions may release high energy. This is why some witches or gypsy fortune tellers – they can hold the thing and see the past. But that don't flow always. Mostly just bounce a bit. It's the atoms retains some things but 'tis dead otherwise."

"Yes, I have always felt that antiques hold a certain something. My boyfriend loved them. We browsed antique shops everywhere we went. He seemed to be able to tell, just by touching something whether it was genuine or not. And he was always right and called out the reproductions."

"Yes Miss, he must have had heightened senses also, Miss!"

"It would be better if I could materialise and show myself to Jane, Miss. Then she would feel more confident. Just using the trees and whispering to her makes her doubt if she ain't just hearing the voices in her own head. If she sees me, Miss, it'll make her more confident."

"Why can't you materialise then? There is plenty of energy about, I am sure you wouldn't get stuck out in the woods for a night. And, I thought that as she is sensitive, being a potential witch, then it wouldn't take much for her to see you if you only materialised a bit?"

"Yes - it would be easy to do that – but I can't do it... let her see me."

"Why? Do you still feel shy in her presence?"

"Sort of Miss, but not sort of, too. I trust her, Miss, and I'm not shy to talk to her. But just look at me, Miss."

"All I see in front of me is an extremely handsome young man, Edward. I am sure that is what Jane will see, too."

"Not me looks, Miss, but me clothes. These ones don't fit properly, I out-growed 'em afore I passed, Miss. I don't want her to think I am all common loike."

"But Arthur and I have talked about this, Edward, you can wear any clothes you want to."

"Only if you can imagine them, Miss. These is the only clothes I can remember. They is hand-me-downs from my bigger brother, Miss. When I first had them they were way too big for me and I looked stupid, Miss. People used to laugh when they saw me. Then I growed just right for them and I was 'appy, Miss. Then I got too big for 'em. Then I got kicked in the 'ead by a 'orse called Maisy, Miss!"

"Aren't there any clothes around the house which you could imagine into, Edward?"

"Not that I would wear, Miss. Well the last fellow here was too tall. His friend who used to stay sometimes – some of 'is clobber is still about but wouldn't wear it. They was hateful fellows. Even Arthur says they didn't deserve the house. I did try to imagine wearing the same clothes as Arthur once, but he is a bit portly, Miss, though don't tell 'im I said that, and 'is clothes they just flapped around me."

"OK, I am going to have to have a think about this one and who knows, maybe we can make you a new outfit, Edward."

"Thank you, Miss, much appreciate it as I do!"

"What did the witch give you to give Jane?"

"Wells, I got a few bits, which I can't give to her all at once. But this book is the first one I gotta give." He indicated an old small wooden box and levitated out a small soft-leather bound book with a leather thong clasp.

"Wow," I said. "May I see?"

"Yes, Miss. She never told me to never show it to no other ghost, Miss."

We levitated it onto the workbench and the thong unfolded and the pages opened. It was so obviously a book of spells with diagrams of all sorts of shapes, numbers, words and pictures which looked like they had been wood-block engraved and printed.

"Double, wow! This must be hundreds of years old."

"Yes Miss, and it has more energy in it than the whole of this house. More energy than I ever felt in anything else made by the living."

I nodded. I could feel it too.

"How she is going to understand it I am not sure though. I can't make head nor tails of it."

"There is some notes on pages folded in the back, Miss. To get her started. It wos the old witch, Mistress Gunn, what wrote them."

"Good luck to that. I tried to learn German once and thought that was bad enough, but this is going to be harder than that," I said.

I realised that Edward appeared slightly upset at this last statement and I looked at him.

"Then there is the rocks, Miss and the trees; and then there is *me*, also, Miss!"

"Oh, of course there is, Edward. How silly of me. Jane is in the safest of hands possible. I am so sorry for not thinking."

Edward relaxed and said, "That's alright, Miss."

"So you are seeing Jane, tomorrow aren't you, Edward?"

"Yes, Miss. Why?"

"Come on, stay close to me, we're going shopping."

A few moments later we materialised outside what obviously looked like, to Edward, a huge shop.

"Wow, Miss. I never saw a shop like this afore. Are we in London Miss? I never been to London afore."

"No Edward. This is Wroxham."

Edward looked puzzled, "Wroxham, Miss? I knowed Wroxham, Miss. This don't look like Wroxham, Miss!" he needed to reassure himself so he quickly zipped his spirit around the town in a matter of seconds as only us ghosts can do.

"I am still a bit puzzled, Miss!"

"Why is that?" I asked.

"Well, Miss. I seen some things, small things still the same, and I remembered a few trees – which used to be a lot smaller. But the thing I can't fathom, Miss, is that this Building 'as a sign says 'Roys of Wroxham' Miss? I used to know 'Roys', but it was in Coltishall then, Miss, and if my mind is correct, Miss, then this ain't Coltishall. Neither ain't it Wroxham, Miss. This should be Hoveton! Whoever, named it, Miss, well they gone and got their geography back-to-front so they 'as. Wroxham 'tis other side of river, Miss."

"Yes, Edward. You are perfectly right. It is Hoveton, but they have always called this 'Roys of Wroxham'. Who knows why? Let's just say it's a 'Norfolk thing'."

"Well, like my mother said, 'There ain't none so strange as Folk'," said Edward, scratching his head.

"Come-on, it's closed up now as it is past 6pm. We can go in and shop 'til we drop!"

We wafted up to the first floor clothing section and spent about an hour searching out clothes to Edward's size. When we had a few bits that he liked we both materialised so that he could try them on and see himself in the mirror. He was really taken by a hooded sweat-shirt which had a stylised skull and cross-bone on the back. I got him to try on as many items of clothing as he would.

"You never know when a change of clothes could come in handy," I told him. "Having this experience will help you to appear in a few bits of gear."

"Yes, Miss, and we're not stealing them Miss, so it isn't a bad thing we're doing."

"Not stealing exactly, just copyright infringement, I guess."

"Is that bad, Miss?"

"Only for the living, not for us ghosts. We can do what we jolly well like, Edward."

"Yes Miss!" We both laughed.

Chapter 12

The seduction of Josh

The next day Josh arrived a bit earlier than the time he normally came and I was hopeful that if Tina did turn up then he would have left by then. Strangely, the first thing he checked was the picture which had fallen off the wall. Luckily none of us had moved it from its position. He picked it up and held it as if deep in thought for a moment. I thought, maybe he is sensitive to ghosts? After all he and Tilly had been friends for years. "Maybe, he can sense that we are here?" I spoke to Edward. He and Tilly were about to take up their positions in the room.

"No, Miss. He is looking for ghosts in a way. But it is his mother he is thinking of when he thinks of spirits. That is why he draws here. 'E wants her to be proud of his talent. 'E don't knows that she passed straight, Miss. He don't understand that. What 'e really is sensing is not 'er but the distant memories of when he lived here. Some of the atoms of the place held onto these memories."

Next Josh sorted some of his sketch book and drawing equipment and laid it out on the table. He then took out another book, with the title, 'Drawing The Live Figure', opened it to reveal black and white photos of nudes. He propped it up against some books from the room so that he could see the photos therein. With a pair of bulldog clips he secured the pages to the backboards of the hard-cover binding. The book wasn't what I had expected. It looked old. The models in it looked as if they had been photographed in the 1920's, judging by the hair styles and fashion layout. Strangely, the women in it were completely naked but the men all wore thongs to cover their private parts.

Josh then produced a series of excellent sketches, starting out with quick sketches and then settling into longer and more detailed workings. This went on for about 2 hours.

Tilly's head shot up. "She is here," she said with distaste. Then a few seconds later I sensed Tina making her way through the hole in the fence. Josh remained totally unaware as to what was happening. Tilly then spoke again. "This is boring, I am going to play down by the brook, Mama," and before I had a chance to say goodbye – she had vanished.

Josh was totally unaware of Tina's presence until she was at the parlour door. When she spoke he nearly jumped out of his skin.

"What are you doing?" she asked – with a seductive slur to her tone. Rather than the black skirt and boots she had worn the last time she was in a comely, summer dress which actually made her look quite attractive.

Josh turned suddenly to face her and defensively said, "I am so sorry, I didn't know anyone was here. Is this your place now? We used to live here once. I am not doing anything."

He was extremely nervous. Tina walked over to him, "No – it isn't my place. I am just out for a stroll in the countryside and thought I heard a noise here and so came in," she lied. Then she said, "Oh argh! Dirty pictures, you're drawing dirty pics!"

Josh seemed very embarrassed and tried to cover his arms over his sketches and then jumped to shut the book up.

"No, no," said Tina, "Give us a look," as if she was a mother speaking to her youngster.

"Oh, I say, they are quite good really. Pity they are not in colour. But good all the same."

"Thank you," answered Josh. He then proceeded to put his drawings away as if he intended to go.

"Why do you copy from a book though?"

"Well, I am at college at the moment. I am hoping to go to Uni after and they do real life drawing on the art course I wanna do. I don't want to look like I haven't done it before."

"So why don't you use a real model?"

"Well, we will at Uni, but that is OK as the costs are covered by the fees. At the moment I couldn't afford a real model and the only life drawing group around here is in Norwich. I can't get there and back in the evenings that easily. So I just come here and sketch from the book." He nodded towards the book and then proceeded to put it in his satchel.

"You off then?"

"Yes, I'd better be going."

"That's not very polite, leaving a young lady in the lurch when we've only just met. We've not even been probably introduced. I am Tina by the way," and she reached out her hand.

'Young' I thought? 'You're almost old enough to be his mother.'

Josh precariously balanced his sketch book half-way into his satchel, a couple of pencils dropped to the floor, as he reached back to shake Tina's hand.

"I am Josh," he replied. Still very nervous.

"Nice to meet you, Josh. A fine handsome boy like you, should stay and have a chat, rather than leaving a lady in the lurch."

I inwardly winced.

Edward got up. He looked a lot more confident in his new clothes. "Right Miss, I'm off," he said, "I have enough energys at the moment and I have to get that Witch book to Jane."

"See you later, Edward, have fun. You look very handsome in your new clothes."

He beamed with pride.

"Thanks, Miss," he said.

Josh replied to Tina, "I really think I must be going."

Tina gave him a sulky look and then suddenly brightened. "I know what. I could be your model. My fella always wanted a dirty picture of me."

Give us a break, I thought. Anyway it should be 'fellas', it should be plural.

Josh seemed to hesitate. "It wouldn't be a dirty picture. I would make it very artistic. I couldn't pay though, that's the problem."

"I'll do it for free, young man. Just let me have one of the pictures you do. So I could give it to my fella."

"I wouldn't know where to draw you, I haven't a studio..."

"We could do it here."

Suddenly Arthur appeared beside me. "Fill me in on what is occurring," he said. It was just then I realised that Patrick was crouched down behind some ivy which crept over the patio windows. He moved as he sniffed the air and I distinctly heard him whisper to himself, "Pipe tobacco, I can smell that pipe tobacco again."

I brought Arthur up to speed on events. He was pleased that Tilly had gone off to play by the brook.

"Well," Josh hesitated. I could sense a wave of excitement come over him. Colour came to his cheeks and it appeared as if he was responding to any pheromones that Tina might have been giving off. "Well, when do you, I mean when would you be available, to model?"

"Well, no time like the present," she said, not giving him time to think. "I'll go grab a sheet from one of the cupboards upstairs and you get your stuff out and set your easel up – or whatever it is you do. I can lie on the sheet when it's over the sofa."

She quickly left and returned with a sheet in a few minutes. Josh had barely had time to get his equipment out and was dropping a lot of it on the floor in nervous anticipation.

Tina threw the sheet over the sofa and lifted her dress over her head. "Here lad, you unhook my bra for me." She turned her back to him.

Josh looked in stunned awe. I don't think that he had expected her to remove her dress in such quick time. His hands fumbled forward and he tried unsuccessfully to unclip the bra. He almost melted when he touched Tina's skin. The smell of her perfume seemed to intoxicate him. Tina got impatient.

"Oh, give us 'ere," she said sharply and reached around her back with both hands and unclipped her bra.

She turned to face him. Her breasts bounced slightly in the turn. "Oh, you've not done this 'afore 'ave thee?" she said more sympathetically.

He shook his head, staring down at her naked breasts. Stunned into silence.

"Ahh, that's sweet," she purred. She took his left hand and motioned across her right breast. Letting it stroke her hard nipple.

"You can't draw what you ain't touched. That's what I always says. Right, you can pull me knickers off now."

Josh appeared to be on automatic pilot and knelt down in front of Tina and pulled her panties down. She hopped out of them.

Arthur turned to me and whispered. "You have to admit it, she is good."

I nodded agreement. "She is. I don't think this is the first time she has gone through this initiation process. I always remember an interview on TV with an elderly John Betjeman. He said that his biggest regret in life was not having more sex when he was younger. Although I no longer have those urges, I sometimes wish that I had an ounce of the confidence in that department, that Tina seems to have. Who knows, maybe things would have turned out differently?"

"All in the past, Lass. Save it up for your next life. Everything will come about."

I nodded again.

Tina suddenly leapt back onto the sofa and said, "Well how do you want me, Josh?"

This seemed to jolt Josh out of his stupor. He asked her to sit with one arm along the back of the sofa. Resting her back against the left arm of the chair whilst feet up, in profile to his position as artist. He then, quickly began to sketch.

After a few minutes Tina became fidgety. "I'm bored. Is it done yet, can I see it?"

Josh told her that it had been hardly anytime at all and that he needed to finish it. Tina started pouting and complaining that she was so bored and she had been sitting for ages – when in reality only about ten minutes had passed.

Eventually, she couldn't wait any longer and jumped up and went around the side of where Josh was sitting. She looked over his shoulder. She seemed disappointed. "It is alright, but it isn't really sexy, is it?"

"I think that I caught your likeness, but I need a few more minutes to finish some of the details."

He turned to her and then realised that her groin was level with his face and so he quickly turned back again. She leaned her groin over his shoulder and started to rock gently against him. "You can finish that after," she told him.

"After...?" he asked puzzled. She rubbed the side of his head gently with one hand and brought her mouth down and started to nibble at his ear lobe.

Josh gave in to her as she took the lead and guided him in the ways of love-making. She dragged him over to the sofa.

"And they're off," said Arthur, as if he was commentating the beginning of a horse race.

Whilst they got on with it, Arthur turned to me and said, "I saw Edward from a distance earlier. What the hell is he wearing! Good Lord. At first I thought we had a new ghost come to join the family. He is hardly recognisable."

I told him about our shopping trip.

"So it is all down to you again? Changing things where they don't need to be changed. If it ain't broke, don't fix it, my girl! Edward now looks like some mad monk with demonic pirate marks over his back."

"Please, Arthur, don't say anything condescending to him and burst his bubble at the moment. He really needs his confidence building-up. He is working really hard to try to get Jane up-to-speed in the ways of witchcraft. If you upset him now then he could be set back and not succeed. Please let him do what he wants!"

He gruffed and said, "Whatever. And, how's all that with Jane going? Are there any problems on the horizon we should be worried about?"

"No, it all seems fine, so please don't upset the apple-cart by criticising how he likes to dress."

"Oh, alright, I swear I shan't say a dicky-bird!"

"Thanks, Arthur. So I take it you don't mind me taking Tilly shopping sometime as well then?"

"Damn and blast it! That girl had more clothes in her lifetime than most members of a Royal Family. Almost every time she appears she is wearing something different. You can't go spoiling her by getting her even more!"

"She really wants to go since she has seen Edward's new clothes. It would be unfair not to take her. Besides, a girl has to keep up with the latest fashions."

Arthur gruffed into his pipe.

I then started to tease him by pretending to pat his belly. "You sure you don't want come shopping too? Looks like you could do with something a little larger," I joked.

"What, what? I'll have you know, my girl, that I haven't put on an ounce of weight since I passed. I believe that I am in pretty good shape for a ghost of my age. Let's see if you can still say the same in 50 years' time." I laughed, and before long he was laughing too.

After a little while Arthur pointed his pipe stem at the window. "Now that's a bit strange don't you think?"

Patrick was watching Tina and Josh still and was masturbating intensely.

"It is but it isn't. I think that the living are shocking me less and less, each day. Before I passed, I would have been dumbfounded to come across such a scene. Now I am starting to take things in my stride. As an auto-mobile analogy goes, he is just tinkering around under the bonnet."

"Yes, and I know we all did it. Some more than others. But it seems strange watching him going at it so much. What I wouldn't give for Suhaib to roll-up now and tap him on the shoulder and inform him that he is trespassing."

I jocularly said, "He would probably ask him if he needed a hand with anything. Patrick would reply, 'No, I am fine matey, everything in hand here'!"

We both laughed at this. Then Arthur said, "Oh, I just remembered, I did see something like it before. Corporal Theakston, yes that was it.1917, France that was.

We had the nurses' latrines set away from the men's. They were screened off by a large, green, canvas supported on wooden stakes stuck into the ground at intervals. It was only meant to be temporary until we could build a more permanent wooden structure. The women didn't seem to mind though. They knew that the war wasn't going well for us at that time and so they were prepared for a little hardship. One young assistant nurse had put out some gossip that if there were permanent loos then that would just be a 'jolly-good target for Jerry to shell'. Anyway, this corporal Theakston had decided to go around to a blind side of the canvas screen and roll a barrel there. He then proceeded to climb up and peer over the top and to do the business, same as what old Patrick is doing there," he gestured with his pipe towards the window.

"Well that is awful," I said. "Were the women upset?"

"Well I don't think that they noticed him that much. Until that is, right at the point of you know, the climax, he got so excited he leaned forward, the bottom of the upturned barrel gave way and he fell full force onto the canvas. Everything, the canvas and stakes that is, went down like a ton of dominoes. Suddenly, no more screen and about 5, naked pink bums jump up from the thunder boxes! The women screamed – I think they thought they had been hit by a shell - and the whole camp looked in their direction. Outcome for that was lots of red faces for days afterwards, lots of innuendos and lewd jokes, and Corporal Theakston lost a stripe!"

I laughed, picturing it all, Arthur made me feel that I had been there in person.

"I think you have warped Patrick, Arthur."

"What do you mean, my dear?" he asked puzzled.

"I was thinking, that similar to Pavlov's dogs salivating when they hear a bell rung at dinner time, Patrick will now get an erection every time he smells pipe tobacco!" We laughed again.

"By the way, what happened with young Jane and the other two ghost-busters? Did she get into a lot of trouble for losing that film?"

"Apparently, she got the sack, they were so angry. Mitch told her that she didn't understand the first thing about Paranormal Seeking. That she had messed up an opportunity to work and learn from the best in the field."

"Was she upset, do you think?"

"No, Edward said that they telephoned her a few days later and told her that as long as she promised not to mess up again and not to try and be a smart-arse then she could join them on a trip to North Wales to explore some abandoned houses there."

"Oh, right, so she is shooting off to Wales and seeking out ghosts there, then?"

"No. According to Edward she told them that 'they could go and do one!' Though Edward wasn't entirely sure what she meant by that!"

"I think we know though, don't we girl? She is a smart lass, that one."

"Edward seems to think so," I replied and we turned our attention back to the shenanigans, which appeared to have come to an end.

Josh was nestling, and cuddling Tina, who seemed a tad frustrated that she hadn't gotten her desired outcome. On the other hand, Josh looked like he had just fallen in love for the first time.

"That was beautiful," he genuinely told her.

"First time, eh. Well second's often better."

"Didn't you enjoy it?"

"It was fine," she said. "Probably best you run along now. My fella will probably be along soon wondering where I got to."

"Oh, gosh, I didn't realise, he was around here, somewhere, with you. I shouldn't have done this. I feel so guilty now."

"Don't worry yourself, lovey, He won't mind. We have, what you might call, an er, 'open relationship'. You run along now though."

"Can I see you again?"

"Yes – same time next week. And try to eat a couple of eggs before you come. To get your strength up loike!"

"Next week? I can't wait. And I will do a more beautiful drawing of you then."

"Oh yes, the drawing. Probably best we cut that bit out, eh love, and get straight on with the other? After all I am happy with the drawing you done already. Sometimes, you can have too much of a good thing can't you, lovey?"

I thought, 'what a bitch'.

Josh got his stuff together and left.

Patrick wandered in from outside.

"Wherever you been?" she asked.

"Watching, outside, like you told me to."

"Well, come here and finish me off. I feel like I just done two rounds with a limp-piece of lettuce. I need something stronger inside of me."

"I can't. Not at the moment, anyway."

"What do you mean you can't?"

"I just knocked it out, out there," he said pointing to the patio doors.

"You what? You selfish git, so you are! You're supposed to do me, not the five-fingered widow! What am I supposed to do? I ain't going back without a good seeing to!"

"Well, give me about half an hour and I'll be up for it again."

Tina seemed so frustrated she appeared livid. "In the meantime you can get on your knees and use your tongue for more than just yapping!" she yelled at him.

"But that's sloppy-seconds!" he whined.

"Floor, knees, NOW!" she commanded him.

He reluctantly got down. And started to ease her frustration.

To try and turn her on, he started talking when he could get his breath.

"So what was it like to have a young buck inside ye?"

"Alright at first, young body and all, but he is so green around the gills. I prefer someone with a bit more zest. With him I had to do all the work. I got, at one point, to hoping that you would come in and smack him over the back of his 'ead with a brick or something."

Patrick stopped. "And why would I do that?"

"Dunno, just jealous rage or something. You doing something passionate like that really turns me on."

"Well the thought of me doing 20-30 years inside, that don't get me none too passionate."

"Only if they found his body!"

I looked at Arthur. He returned a worried look to me.

"Is this another fantasy?" asked Patrick.

"Why, does it turn you on?"

"If it is a fantasy, it could turn me on. If it is the real thing then I am for 'jogging-on', as you said. I ain't ready for jail-time."

"OK, it's a fantasy."

"What do you want me to do then?"

"Just imagine, we were – me and him – going at it. And he is just gonna climax and you rushed in and whacked 'im one?"

"What if I crept in with a rope and strangled 'im?"

"Ohh argh, go on!"

"Well, he'd be a bit like a bucking bronco. He would start thrashing about, pushing deeper and deeper into you as the life ebbed outta him!"

Tina started moaning, "God, you're making me cum. I'm coming."

Just then we felt a massive charge of energy in the room. It seemed all of a sudden to be dark. I looked around and there was the dark shadowy figure of Devlin pointing his gnarled finger at me. "Witch," he rasped at me. Arthur got between me and him and shouted at him to begone.

Devlin chuckled, "You don't scare me, you weak ghost. Begone yourself."

"I am warning you!" cried Arthur.

I felt energy being drained from myself, and I knew the same was happening to Arthur.

"Warn away you fool," Devlin rasped back.

"Angela, resist him. He can't hurt us. We see the bigger picture. Focus on the bigger picture. He is just a pointless ghost who walks the earth. He has wandered so long that he has become a demon. We have seen the other side. We know of what comes."

I started to do as Arthur told me, focusing upon the light at the end of the tunnel and the voices.

Devlin saw that we were resisting. He turned and looked at the two lovers. He made a move towards them and went in through Patrick and into the body of Tina.

Tina started going crazy with lust. She started screaming at Patrick to hurt her. He slapped her. Then she started saying, "Yes, we could do it. Soon – let's corrupt his soul first. Next week we'll get him involved with other things. When the time is right we'll kill the little shit, Not a fantasy. You come up behind him and slit his throat. I want to feel the gush of his blood over my naked body as he loses his life and I orgasm. You wouldn't deny me an orgasm, would you, Patrick?"

Suddenly, Devlin appeared in Pat's body as well. Pat's eyes turned red. He had a huge demonic grin on his face. "No, I won't deny you, my love. We won't get caught, we can burn this hovel down and they will never have any evidence that we were here." At that they both orgasmed.

Devlin came out of their bodies and stared at Arthur for a brief moment. He laughed and said to Arthur, "You, you fool, you won't intervene as you don't believe in meddling. And you my dear," he addressed me, "you, I have already dealt with in the past. That was easy enough and so I won't expect a fight from you. And, at the moment I am also having a great time messing with that ex-boyfriend of yours. Messing up his mind. I will soon drive him crazy!" With that, he disappeared.

Tina and Patrick lay exhausted on the sofa. Bodies entwined in sweat and other fluids.

"What was that about, Arthur?" I pleaded. "Why did he say he was trying to drive my ex-boyfriend mad?"

"Ignore him, my dear. He is just playing games with *your* mind. If you let him get the better of you, then you will be the mad one. That is his goal. To weaken you so that he can enter your soul."

But I couldn't get that last statement out of my mind. If Devlin hated me then he shouldn't be allowed to hurt the ones around me, to further hurt me. After this last episode, and seeing how he manipulated Tina and Patrick for his wickedness, I was sure of something though. I knew in my heart that this horrible demon was the main protagonist in my very own death.

I turned to Arthur and almost shouted in panic, "We must intervene. We have to save Josh."

I expected him to counter with an argument about destiny taking its own course and fate not being our responsibility. But instead of that, something marvellous happened.

Before my eyes Arthur changed. He manifested no longer as a pipe-smoking elderly man, as he previously had. He grew stronger. Looked younger. His clothes changed. He stood before me, strong, shoulders back, chest out. He had become a Captain again in his first World War Uniform. From his stiffened peak cap to his puttees and down to his ammunition boots. Arthur projected every bit the young man that Nicole and Irene had loved. His brass buttons seemed to shine, even though they were blackened down for camouflage. A leather strap across his chest met with his belt at the point where a pistol hung in a brown leather holster. His thick woollen khaki tunic and trousers looked like no bullet would ever be able to pierce them. A silver whistle hung from one of his pockets.

When he spoke, his voice seemed younger. The same Arthur, but firmer, more sure.

"Yes, my dear, time for action. That cad has overstepped the mark. We're now officially at war!"

I suddenly felt so full of confidence and proud of him. He was our World War 1 hero. He was the one to lead us into battle.

We ignored Tina and Patrick as they dressed. They were insignificant vassals of a demented demon. We were the ghosts. We had seen the other side. Together we could defeat the three of them.

I suddenly had an idea.

Patrick yelped, "Oh!"

"What's the matter with you?" Tina asked. "Twice in one day too much for you, is it?"

He held the side of his head. "I just felt something pull my hair," he whined.

"You, Big Girl's Blouse," said Tina. "You hardly have any hair left to pull. You probably just got it caught on something, or was bitten by a bug."

I had retained a few of Patrick's hairs. The new Arthur looked at me curiously. I put my finger up to my mouth in a sign that it was a secret. He tapped the side of his nose, and winked. "Mum's the word," he said.

Tina and Patrick left the building.

Chapter 13

Organising and resistance

After the two of them had left I stood back, still in awe of Arthur's transition.

"You look amazing," I exclaimed. "Can I give you a hug?"

"Whatever. Get it over with though, we've got things to be getting on with. Planning and the such-like!" He manifested solid enough so that I could manifest and put my arms around him, and squeezed him to me.

I sensed the smell of gun oil, leather, and surgical cleaning fluid. But not pipe tobacco. Maybe a whiff of cigarette smoke. His brass buttons and whistle pressed into my chest. I also felt the overwhelming sense of security and protection. I stood back and gave him an admiring look.

"I can't smell your pipe any more."

"Well, no you wouldn't. Didn't start until 1919 – after I got back!"

I stood and looked at the sight of him again.

"You look amazing Arthur. Every inch a hero."

"Whatever, my dear. Just a bit of clobber I used to wear. Nothing special!" He seemed slightly abashed from my hug. As if he was embarrassed by the intimacy of it.

"What's the whistle for? Is that when you used to lead your men over-the-top?"

"Good Lawd, no, me dear. I never went over-the-top. I was a Doctor. Kept safe in the rear echelon. Safe apart from the shelling and snipers, that is. The whistle is for stretcher bearers, to summon them. They knew my call a mile away. Some of them that whistled for men to go-over-the top weren't always heroes. Some of them were upper-class idiots who never shot a Bosch in their lives. Used their pistol as if it were a tool to herd cattle, so they did. I patched up many a wound where the fellow said that it was inflicted by his own officer because he had tried to turn around and go back to the safety of the trench.

"That is really terrible," I said, "but I did hear of such things happening, in a documentary I watched on TV."

"Don't get me wrong, dear. Not all officers were dastardly. A lot were very gallant and gave their lives for others, without an inkling that they would pass over as we know. Some of them just thought of death as a full-stop. Nothing beyond. They were real heroes. But some, they just thought of their men as lower-class cattle, or sheep even. Just to be herded and used, like balls on a billiard table. And they thought that they were the cue to pot the shot. And shoot they did. Their own men. Blast them, and their egos. Most must have felt some shame when they eventually passed and realised that we're all the same really. Cut from the same cloth!"

"Unfortunately, not a lot has changed. We still have those sorts of people in the world. Often so rich that they don't know what to do with their wealth and so they play with the lives of others. That is a bit of what the rock told me. Karma comes about," I lamented.

"Karma is a natural balance, my girl. Most of those sorts will probably be sent back to become creatures again. To see life from a bug's angle. Looking up at the sole of a boot."

"So, in a way there is a hell then?"

"Yes, I suppose there is. But not one that Dante envisaged. Not like in the Gustave Dore images."

I had seen those images myself. My boyfriend had a book from around 1890, with the illustrations in, and so Arthur didn't need to explain further.

"So there is some form of justice then?"

"In the after-life, yes. But don't get me going on justice for the living."

He continued, "After I had passed, and after I had, mostly, gotten over my fear of the living, I had a hobby of popping down to Norwich Crown Court, as a fly-on-the-wall, so to speak. I sat in on many trials there. Ghosts can always tell when people are lying. Much more than judges can. Let me tell you. There are more uneducated people in prison. Not because they commit more crimes. It is because they say the wrong things at the wrong time. Confess when they feel pressured. Or they can't afford the right lawyer who can advise them what to say and what not to say.

"Many a sanctimonious Judge has gone home feeling pleased with themselves, when in fact they have banged the wrong person up or let a wrong 'un off! Many a drink has been bought for them in the golf clubs and private hotels, the world over, by people who should be serving time. There is no real justice for the living. And others are going through their own hell. By serving time for things they dinnae do. Not that a lot didn't deserve banging-up. The world needs to be kept safe and have some order. But I believe that a lot who could afford it, got off scot-free.

"Wouldn't that be the fault of the Jury, rather than the Judge?"

"What, my girl? Twelve people, most often eight of whom are there reluctantly and want to get back to their dreary lives, two there who are keen as mustard for the gossip factor; the last two; a strong one who believes that everybody is guilty and can swing the others to his/her opinion; last one believes in the defendant but in the end is badgered into going with the flow. The verdict very often lies with the Judge's summing-up. And they are not always impartial.

"It's not always about what you know or who you know. Sometimes it is just about who you can afford to know!"

"Well, I hope that Karma bites those judges' bums, if that's the case!" I stated.

"I am sure it will my girl. Everything comes around that goes around. Especially for those who feel they can sit in judgement of their fellow men!

But at the end of the day, we still need law and order. And this here, Tina and Patrick ought to be banged up for a few years."

After a moment's reflective pause he said, "Talking about judges, we'll have to set up plan as to how we are going to deal with Devlin and those two psychopathic accomplices. It wouldn't surprise me, now, if he were a judge and not a priest in a previous life."

"I am worried what Tilly will do when she finds out."

He looked at me, concerned, after I had said this.

"Best keep quiet for the moment. We don't need to trouble her just yet. They said that they weren't going to try to kill Josh next week. May never happen. They still have their games to play."

"So, we are going to lie to Tilly?"

"Not lie exactly. Just don't tell her yet. Keep her in reserve. As a secret weapon, so to speak."

"OK, just for now," I agreed, not quite sure that we should look at Tilly as a weapon, even though she was the most powerful amongst us.

"We'll have a meeting, tomorrow – the three of us, you, me and Edward - when Tilly is playing out some time. We can figure out a way to stop this from happening."

"I am so glad that you see that it is right, Arthur. I thought that you were going to say that we couldn't meddle."

"I am obliged to in this case, Angela. I made a promise to Josh's mother when she passed. A promise to look after them both."

The next day an unusual event took place which made Arthur's last statement take further shape. I was standing looking out of one of the upper windows and I saw a man staring through the security fence. At first I was startled and a little scared and quickly withdrew from the window. However, something drew me back to look again. I felt that I recognised him.

Arthur came in the bedroom and smartly walked over to me in his dashing uniform.

"Look at that man," I said pointing, "Do you think he will come in?"

"Him? No, I think not. That is Josh's father, the writer. He stops by every now and then and stares at the place. Probably remembers the time he lived here. Loved his wife dearly. Probably still has a lot of grief."

"I think that he knows my dad. They used to stand and watch our football team when I was playing. Whenever I scored and looked back, often my dad had not seen the goal, because the two of them were engrossed in conversation. Do you think that we could use him to stop Tina and Patrick hurting Josh?"

"No, I very much doubt it. I spent some time following him on the long walks he goes on, just for the company. He treks all over. Miles and miles, he goes. Often ends up sitting in a church for the peace and quiet. Takes out his note book there. He's not religious. I think that it is the only place he can write these days. At one time, years back, he was almost a celebrity in these parts. Lots of columns in the local paper, even did a show on local radio about Norfolk history and stuff. Interesting man but he hasn't the slightest sensitivity for ghosts of anyone I have ever come across. Virtually impossible to communicate with him. So I wouldn't bother trying to rope him in on our 'Plan of attack', so to speak."

"What if we did like Edward did with Jane? Sort of orbed a window and wrote a message on it?"

"Most likely help him pass over a couple of years before he should. Poor fella, would probably have a heart-attack. Weakened like he has been, through years of grief."

"Oh, I never thought of that. Good point."

"Yes, leave him out of our plans. Don't want to worry him too much over his son. I am sure that between us should be able to figure out something."

"Arthur."

"Yes, my girl?"

"I think that I am going to follow him on his walk."

"Pointless, dear. Like I just said you won't be able to communicate with him for all the tea in China. And besides his heart won't take it if you try."

"It's not that. I think it's because I feel that if I follow him, it may lead me to a stage, or the next step in my destiny. I won't try to communicate with him. Girl-Guide's honour," I promised, holding up two fingers as a salute.

"Destiny, eh? Both you and Edward pursuing your destinies now, eh?"

"Did I just hear my name mentioned?" Edward was standing behind us.

Arthur turned to him.

Edward was stunned, "Cripes, did Miss take you shopping too, Arthur?"

"What? Oh, the uniform, see what you mean. No these are some old clothes I put on until we tackle that Demon Devlin. Glad to see that you're back wearing your old clothes again though, young fellow."

"Yes, why are you back in your old clothes again? Did they get wet in the brook, Edward?" I asked him.

"No Miss, no. A ghost's clothes can't ever get wet... Oh you're joking Miss! No, I am back in me old clobber because of Jane, Miss!"

"Why so?"

"Well Miss, I materialised to her and when she saw me, Miss, she was right disappointed, Miss. She said that she had imagined me in Edwardian clothes, Miss. She also said that the clothes I was wearing reminded her of a bully who lives down her road that she used to go to school with, Miss. She said that alls he does all day is get drunk and live off the dole, whatever that be, Miss. So I changed back, and she was ever so pleased, she was."

"Did she like the book?"

"Yes Miss, she is so excited about it. Says that she has had dreams of it afore."

"Materialised... book? Seems like I have missed out on some things," gruffed Arthur.

"Seems I have, too," said a more confident Edward. "Why are we taking on the demon, does Tilly know?"

"Look Arthur, can you fill Edward in on what happened with Tina and Josh, and the part about Tilly? I am sure that Edward can also talk to you about Jane so that you are reassured. And another thing, Edward."

"Yes Miss?"

"I think that we may need to bring Jane in on our mission, to protect Josh."

"But we have not discussed that, my girl," stammered Arthur.

"Look, I haven't got time at the moment, I need to follow Josh's dad and he's leaving."

"If you needs to follow someone and you lose them, you can always use the trees, Miss. Any tree, Miss."

"Right, gotta go, if you can both do as I asked I'd much appreciate it. I'll be back as soon as I can."

Arthur clipped his heels together and saluted, "Seems I am not the most senior-ranking officer here after all," as he winked at Edward. I gave him a cheeky grin and left.

I followed Josh's father for a couple of hours that day. At first the weather was fine, a sunny spring day as we had been getting used to. Then it became overcast and began to rain a bit. Obviously, the rain never concerned me at all. However, I was also surprised that it didn't seem to deter Josh's father either, so lost in thought was he. He ploughed on regardless.

As Arthur had suggested my quarry led us both to a church and he went in and sat on the left-hand side at a pew towards the back. I sat across the aisle and watched whilst he removed a note book from a small backpack and a retractable mechanical pencil from a pocket from the inside of his jacket. Arthur was again correct, in that Josh's Father didn't have any sense of my presence. There were actually a couple of other ghosts attached to this church, and they popped out when they had sensed Josh's father approach. I supposed that they were used to him by now as they relaxed very quickly. One was presented as a very old woman in a shroud, the other a teenaged girl, possibly around 16, with a very pale complexion and darkened eye sockets. I sensed her passing in sickness during the late Victorian era. They indicated a greeting to me. I reciprocated and they went on about what they were doing. They had sensed that I wasn't a permanent feature and that I was just there because of their living visitor.

Josh's father had a very sad demeanour, as befitting his grief I suppose. I felt a bit of pity for Josh. He hadn't only lost his mother when she passed, but also his father. He must have been a lonely young man and I could see why he had succumbed to Tina's seductive web so easily.

Craving affection to make up for some which has been missing in life is a trait common to a lot of people and can lead to some seeking love in the wrong people and places. I was no psychologist in my previous life, I had been a hairdresser with my own salon, my father had helped setting me up in. But in a way, I felt that most hairdressers get a truer insight into the issues which people deal with on a regular basis. Psychologists have limited clientele. Whereas, nearly everybody needs their hair cut and so hairdressers talk to those who suffer anxieties alongside those who don't appear to ever suffer from issues. I had sometimes thought that psychologists or psychiatrists should spend some time seeing the 'well', and see how they cope with their ups and downs, so that they had a yardstick to judge their other patients by. After all, your outlook would a bit one-sided if you only ever deal with the sick and look for text-book remedies. Note to self, I thought, speak to Arthur about these ideas. As an ex GP he would have some wise thoughts and his opinion would be invaluable, I am sure.

My meandering concentration had left Josh's dad unattended for a couple of moments and when I remembered why I was there I looked to see him staring perplexed at his notebook. I felt so curious as to why he was staring like he was at his notebook that I went over. I looked across his shoulder at his page he had just written. As I read it I became nervously excited. The last paragraph read:

'Try and be a better father to Josh. He needs me and I have been absent whilst wallowing in my own grief. He is a victim of losing his mother and he must also feel that I am not there for him.'

'Question: Can psychologist diagnose a patient correctly for a psychiatrist to treat? After all they only see one side of humanity. Maybe a hairdresser who talks to everyone – the sick and well – would be better able to give the best analysis and guidance?'

Note to self – 'Ask Arthur'.

Josh's dad stared hard at what he had just written. He spoke out loud, thinking he was alone in the church. "Who the hell is Arthur?" he asked nobody in particular.

Then he said out loud, "He is a doctor! I believe Arthur is a doctor. Not one I have ever met though, whatever part of my brain did I drag him up from? I am definitely going loopy, even talking to myself now!"

I was stunned. He couldn't sense my presence but he must have picked up on my thoughts and translated them to his own writings in way he could interpret. Similar to how the rocks feedback the answers to questions.

"Ha! He has become a medium, my girl!" Arthur stated after I returned and told him what was happening.

"A medium?" I replied.

"Yes - though the way you just said it reminds me of a radio sketch with that music hall comedian, Arthur Askey. I always remember that show he had on the radio, 'A medium, a medium, you say you are, madam? Not from where I am looking you're not! More like a large to me!' He was a comic that man was," Arthur chuckled.

"Arthur Askey? I remember him from Saturday Night at the London Palladium. I think he passed away a couple of years ago, didn't he?" I asked.

"Er, a few more than a couple of years ago, my dear. I think you may have been on the other side for a bit longer than you think."

"Oh, I keep forgetting," I said. "How can Josh's father become a medium? Don't you have to be born with psychic powers?"

"I think that his grief may have triggered the powers. His senses have become overloaded, possibly. Like the tyres on an auto-mobile, the more they race about, the thinner the rubber gets. He had no ability to pick up on anything when he lived here in this house. At that time he was completely devoid of spirit. From what you have told me, his writing has developed into a tool."

"A tool? I don't understand."

"Well certain mediums – real ones – can walk in a room and sense those – like us – who have passed. Others need to use tools. There are some, for instance who can draw the features of the dead without ever having seen their face or a photo. Then a relative may recognise them.... With Mr. O'Connell, his writing has become his tool. It is termed automatic writing. Lots of mediums used this as a tool to pick up messages. What you were thinking didn't 100% correspond to what he wrote. That is common. There is a bit of insulation and delayed reactions which take place. It isn't a direct line of communication you know and therefore open to interpretation!"

"Oh, is that his and Josh's surname, O'Connell? I think I have heard my dad say that name a few times."

"Yes, that's it, girl!"

"I am pleased that Mr. O'Connell didn't pick up on my thoughts of Tina seducing his son."

"He may have, my girl. But when we are living, if thoughts like that flash through the mind about the ones we love, we quickly dismiss them, or push them to the back of the mind where they become mere hunches."

"So anyone can become a medium then?"

"Given the right situation and context, I suppose so, yes."

"Should I use this communicating method, automatic writing, to warn him about Josh's safety?"

"I wouldn't for the moment. He doesn't yet know what it is he is doing. It would take him time to understand his gift. If he is not told by other experienced mediums and taught how to use his 'gift' then he may go into overdrive and feel he has lost his mind. Many a failed spiritualist there are in the mental hospitals up and down the country."

"They refer to them as psychiatric hospitals these days."

"I wonder how many of them they have in Constantinople," he replied, half mocking.

"Names, and what we call things, seem to keep changing, Arthur. Don't blame me, I am just the messenger. Anyway, if I have been away so long, they might have changed what they call psychiatric hospitals, altogether again. So don't quote me on anything. Next week they'll probably be calling a goose a gander, or vis-versus!" At the time I didn't realise how true this last statement would come to pass.

Chapter 15

The second seduction of Josh

Tina got there early, Josh also got there early. Early to their rendezvous date. They were both eager to resume what had occurred before. Tina, because of expectations of the future, and Josh, because of expectations of the past. Tina was the first to arrive about ten minutes before-hand with Patrick in tow. Tina had brought a bag with a couple of clean sheets. She gave one to Patrick and put the other one under her arm.

Tilly eyed them suspiciously. She was disappointed in the obvious fact that Tina was there, and there was obviously going to be no drawing today. "I am going to play," she said to the rest of us, and disappeared without her usual goodbyes. We all felt a bit of relief at this. When we had discussed further courses of action, earlier we thought that this might occur. Nonetheless we did feel a bit nervous about keeping her out of the loop as to what was going on. Maybe, she sensed this from us. Her senses were so much more powerful than ours and I really didn't want to let her down, or upset her in any way.

"Right, remember what we discussed, I'll get him started and bring him up to the room when he is comfortable enough," Tina told Patrick.

"How long will that be?" he asked.

"I don't bloody know, do I? I will only know that when he is so horny, he can't say 'no'."

Arthur had been looking down his peaked cap at them both as if they were low-life, new recruits. I shot him a worried glance.

"Are they going to try to murder Josh today, do you think?" I asked him with a feeling akin to panic.

"No," he stated assuredly. "They have emptied the bag of what they brought with them and there was no knife with them. I believe it is as they discussed last week. They are just trying to taint his soul somehow. They are playing their games."

"Well, I hope that they don't try to hurt him today as we haven't planned for that."

"I wouldn't have thought that hurting him today would be part of their game plan. If they still wanted to murder him, then they wouldn't get him to come back the next time if they hurt him today. He simply wouldn't turn up again – I am sure."

I saw the logic in this statement. But, even so, I didn't want to be wrong-footed and caught out by unexpected actions on their part.

"Right, I am off upstairs then," said Patrick.

"That is what I told you, didn't I? Oh, and another thing. Don't knock one out up there. I don't want to get upstairs to find you all limp, like!"

"Right, I am going upstairs to follow this miscreant, you stay here and keep an eye on proceedings. And Eddy my boy, if need be you can pop between the two of us," instructed Arthur.

"Righto Sir!" said Edward.

I flicked my two backward finger Girl-Guide salute, up to my forehead, as confirmation.

Josh looked like he had made a special effort and was a lot smarter in appearance than the last time I had seen him. His hair was brushed and I imagined he had showered before-hand and probably distributed deodorant and talc about his body. He also wasn't carrying his satchel of drawing equipment. He hurried in as if he didn't expect Tina to be here and was visibly relieved when he saw her sitting on a newer sheet over the sofa.

Tina was wearing her old black leather skirt and fish-net stockings with a black lace, see-through top and no bra. Josh was affected straight away by her appearance. Tina had known he would be. She beckoned him to come over to her and, when he was within range pulled him onto the sofa and started to snog his face off. Josh just went with the flow. He appeared slightly more confident than the first time and seemed less docile. I thought that he had probably thought about this a lot in the intervening week. He might even have done some research through pornographic resources. I remembered a friend telling me that her boyfriend had confessed to her of doing this before his first time. Or maybe he had just had two eggs that morning, as Tina had suggested he do.

After about 20 minutes of tongue-kissing and caressing, Tina suddenly stopped and sat up. Josh looked concerned.

"What is it, have I done something wrong?" he worriedly asked.

"No, lovey. You are actually a bit better than before. No, I just got a nice surprise for you."

"Surprise? What surprise?"

"If I told you then it wouldn't be much of a surprise now, would it? But we need to go up to one of the bedrooms to experience the surprise."

Josh looked uncertain and stood up.

"Can't we stay here? I like it here."

Tina grabbed the loose material of one leg of his trousers and pulled him close – so that her face was level with his groin.

"Come here, soppy ol' you," she purred. Within seconds she had unzipped his flies and grappled his penis out of his pants. She put it in her mouth and began to give him a blow-job. Josh relaxed immediately, and ran his fingers through her hair in ecstatic pleasure. She carried this on for 10 minutes, until he began to moan,

"I'm cumming, I'm gonna cum."

Whereon, she immediately stopped, stood up, grabbed his hand and said, "That's the spirit." She then quickly led him upstairs without giving him time to think.

I materialised next to Arthur who was behind the screen with Edward before they had a chance to reach the room. "What's happening?" I asked.

Arthur replied, "Patrick is just lying on the bed, stark naked, playing with himself again. Not so frantic as the last time, though."

Edward looked a bit bored and was lying on the floor reading a magazine. Well, mostly looking at the pictures, I think.

Tina came into the room. Patrick looked up, hand still on his erect penis. Josh looked stunned. He had entered the room so quickly behind Tina that he was in the middle of the room before he noticed the naked man prostrate on the bed. He turned pale and walked back into the open wardrobe behind him. Deep into the bug infested clothes to hide. Then he reached out a hand and pulled the door shut.

Tina looked frustrated. She spun around to Patrick and spat, "Did you have to go and take your clothes off already?"

"Well, you said I was to get things prepared," he replied defensively.

"I meant get the clean sheet on the bed, you idiot. Not start playing with yourself! You've gone and frightened him now!" Tina was livid.

Then she calmed herself and went over to the wardrobe and tapped on the door. "Josh, don't be silly now. This is only Patrick. He just wants to watch."

"I thought you said I was gonna join in too," whined Patrick.

Tina spun around and wagged her finger threateningly towards Patrick, "Shut-up. Not another f'ing word out of you – or I swear. Just shut-up whilst I fix this, you imbecile."

"Nice lady," I addressed Arthur, "I can see why you used to refer to them as 'The Lovers'. This is true love, this is."

Arthur frowned at me.

"Josh, it's alright. I told you afore, me and him, well we have an open relationship, see. It ain't his fault, Patrick I mean, but he had an accident and the doctor told him it was gonna be difficult for him to have sex. So the doctor said that this might help him."

Patrick looked baffled.

"An accident?" asked a muffled Josh.

"Yes, unfortunate accident," said Tina. "At work one day, one of the forklift drivers came around a corner ever so quick, they did. Well the forks were raised. And Patrick here, well, he got 'is nuts crushed by one of the forks. Since then he has had a lot of difficulty in getting it up, so 'e 'as! Ain't you, Patrick?"

"Yes, yes, that's right, Tina. That's exactly what happened. So the doctor, Josh, 'e suggested a threesome to try to get me right again. If I 'adn't had them crushed I wouldn't be 'ere today, so I wouldn't. It's only on the doc's advice," Patrick called out so that Josh could hear him.

"What credible doctor in their right mind would suggest such a ridiculous thing?" asked Arthur. "Very unprofessional, it sounds to me."

"I think they are making it up, Arthur. Just take it with a pinch of salt!" I told him.

"Oh, I see, my girl!" he replied.

"You're not jealous about me and Tina then, and gonna hurt me?" asked a worried Josh from inside the wardrobe.

"No, mate, no. I think that it is good. I mean I don't want Tina to go without just because I can't do it, now, do I? No, that would make me a very selfish bloke. Wouldn't it now? And besides, you look like a nice lad for 'er to be doing it with."

"Yes, Josh. I told Patrick how nice and gentle you was with me last time and 'e was right pleased 'e was." She had looked at Patrick and raised her eyebrows, as if even she thought she might be stretching the truth a bit far this time.

"OK," said a still, uncertain and nervous Josh.

"Josh?"

"Yes Tina?"

"Do you remember what I was just doing to you downstairs, just now?"

"Yes, Tina."

"Well, if you come out again, I can carry on doing that. It relaxed you didn't it?"

"Yes Tina. It was lovely, it was."

"Well, if you come out. I will do it. You don't need to mind that Patrick is here. It is just a form of medical therapy 'is doctor advised 'im. As harmless as that, so it is."

"OK Tina." Josh spoke quietly, and slowly the wardrobe door opened.

Patrick got up from the bed and went and leaned against an old chest-of-drawers, to make way. He was still fully naked. Tina took hold of Josh's hand and led him out of the wardrobe and over to the bed. She sat down and resumed what she had been doing to Josh downstairs, whilst he stood and started to moan. He avoided any sort of eye contact with Patrick. Probably out of respect for the dominant male in the room, he moaned more quietly than before. I feel he was afraid that if he moaned too loudly he would upset the afflicted Patrick for enjoying something which he couldn't.

In another 10 minutes, or so Tina had removed Josh's clothing as well as her own and they were writhing on the bed. Patrick, five minutes or so later, sat on the edge of the bed and started to stroke both of their bodies with one hand, whilst masturbating with the other.

Then the inevitable happened. Devlin appeared.

"Dam and blast!" shouted Arthur.

"Dam and double blast," I said.

Edward jumped up from his magazine. "Don't worry, I'll deal with 'im," he heroically said and walked through the screen to confront Devlin.

"Oh, it is you, me lad, is it?" asked Devlin of Edward.

"Aye, it is me, sir. And If you would remove yourself from this 'er, building I would be much appreciative – so I would! If you 'member, rightly, you lost in a fight with me and other spirits afore, sir." Edward had braced his whole spiritual persona as one ghost who was up for a fight.

Devlin stood and laughed.

"You're not the one to challenge me alone now, my lad? Do you ever wonder why that mare, Maisy kicked you in the head? That lovely Maisy, who was the horse you loved amongst all others? Ever wonder why she killed ye, do yer bouy? Well I can tell 'e. 'T was 'cause of 'me', my lad. I went into the spirit of a hornet and triggered her hoof. I waited just for the moment. Your head was the target, and when alls was right an' in place and rosey, I stung her in the rump. So I did. I hated your pathetic life, so I did. So soft, always thinking the best of everyone. And the worse thing is.... we're related, you know? You are one of my sister's descendants," he rasped.

Edward began to stammer again, "I knewed it, I did. Maisy wouldna hurt anyone so she wouldn't. Tweren't 'er fault she killed me. I never did blamed 'er anyways. She is just a living creature who don't think like 'people' do. She never meant no 'arm to anyone. I don't ever want to 'ave you as my unc, unc, uncle or cousin!"

Edward's stammering meant that he was quickly losing energy and confidence following this latest revelation from Devlin.

Arthur and I immediately appeared next to Edward, in a show of strength. Devlin hesitated when he saw us three together. He then looked straight at Arthur,

"So new battle-clothes, eh Arthur? Dissatisfied with the way things were? Well, so am I! Disappointed that this here young whipper-snapper, along with you and that girl have decided to meddle this time. It won't end well for thee three!"

He was strong – so powerfully strong. Absorbing all of the energy from the room. I could feel the small creatures around having their colours drained. I am sure a few hundred passed over. All of their energies flowing to Devlin, making him stronger.

"Steady now," came Arthur's calm voice to us. "Don't let him get to you. Absorb some of the power from him. Weaken him. Think of the other side. Draw on the fairness of death. Draw on the truth of passing over. He should have gone a long time ago. Make him weak."

In unison, we lifted our hands in his direction and summoned his energy towards us. It started to work. Meanwhile, the lovers were becoming more frantically engrossed in passion on the bed. Patrick had lain down with Josh and Tina. They were entwined in a writhing mass of sweat and passion. Devlin, suddenly, jumped in amongst them and was absorbed, going from body to body. For a brief moment I saw Josh's eyes flicker with the madness of the possessed. He pushed himself hard into Tina.

"That's it, lad. You're getting it now. Harder, harder," she screamed with passion.

Arthur instructed myself and Edward to stop trying to absorb Devlin's energy, lest we harm Josh accidentally. Our arms dropped to our sides. We looked on helplessly, as Josh was further instructed, and corrupted.

Patrick moved up to the head of the bed and placed his reddened penis in Tina's mouth. She engulfed it as if it were giving her an infusion of energy. Saliva trickled out of the side of her mouth. Josh passionately kissed her neck, and licked his tongue up and over her face so that he licked the flowing juices. Tina grabbed hold of Patrick's penis and placed it in Josh's mouth. I expected him to jump up backwards in shock and fear, but instead he just sucked on it as passionately as Tina had just done. Devlin appeared in Tina.

Tina laughed a sardonic laugh and almost cackled with delight. "Corrupted you are. We will turn you into a pervert, my lad. Tonight you are going to get well and truly fucked!"

She then turned her head towards us and grinned. Juices still dribbling from her lips, like a demented drug addict. But it wasn't Tina looking at us. I could tell – it was Devlin.

Eventually, fully exhausted, the three ceased their motions and lay spent on the sheet. They lay for some time.

Devlin freed himself from them and smiled his ghoulish face at us.

"You can't stop the corruption of this young lad. This is a repeat of past events. People have been corrupted since the dawn of time. It is in their nature to become corrupted. Then, they become my weapon to corrupt others, if I so wish. Otherwise, they can be tossed aside like this young lad will be. His body returned to the worms, *cinerem in cinerem, pulverem in pulverem.*

"I don't believe you. I don't believe that we are going to let you harm this young man!" I shouted towards him.

He just laughed at me in return, then he vanished.

Arthur put a reassuring hand on my arm. "I don't think that Josh is in danger of any harm today. Devlin wouldn't have left if he were. It is as we thought. Next week will be the aim for them," he indicated Tina and Patrick. "Next week, if our plan works, we will scupper their mischievous intentions."

I looked around. It was still early, just after noon. I spoke to Edward, "You are seeing Jane this afternoon, aren't you?" I asked him.

"Yes, Miss, in about an hour's time."

"OK, just ask her if she would be willing to come to the old lady Beech tree at about the same time tomorrow. I want to see if I can communicate with her via the tree. Is that alright, Edward? Do you think she would be up for that?"

"Yes, Miss. She is learning every day, since she had the book. She ain't so wooden now, Miss. Like it was always meant to be. And I thinks that the book is giving her power, like them there batteries Arthur stole off the ghost busters. She is like that tranns'itor radio thingy, which 'as all the music coming outta her. I do believe that afore long she'll be a proper witch."

I gave Arthur a worried glance. Would this mean that we would lose Edward soon if his task was complete? Arthur seemed to understand what I thought.

"I am sure that Edward means by 'before long', is at least 2 years, isn't it right, Edward?"

"Yes, Arthur. But as us ghosts knows, 2-3 years ain't a long-time, is it?" He beamed a confident smile.

"No lad, soon passes, so it does. Soon goes!" Arthur replied.

I felt relief.

"I need to ask Jane to do some tasks for us if she could. Who knows, in the future she may call on us to do things she needs," I told Edward.

"Oh, she ain't like that, Miss. I am sure she would do whatever you asked of her and won't want nothing in return, Miss."

"I hope she can. But what I am going to ask her is going to be unpleasant and she might not want to do it."

"If you's to 'splain to 'er, Miss, that it is a good intention behind it, Miss. I is sure she will trust your judgement good and proper, Miss!"

"I hope so," I said.

As an aside I asked Edward what he had meant about defeating Devlin in the past. He told me about how during World War 2, the occupiers of the house then had taken in a couple of children, evacuees from London.

"There was more ghosts 'ere then, Miss. It was just after Arthur had come – weren't it, Arthur?" Arthur nodded in affirmation.

"Yes, my lad, just after."

"Well, Tilly was here, obviously, then there was Mr. Tankard, the blacksmith, (not all blacksmiths are called Smith, ye knows), and let me think… Oh, Mavis Cartwright. The milkmaid who had been here the longest and knew Devlin's tricks. She was the strongest ghost I ever met. Well it was her mostly cast Devlin out on 'is ear."

"What was he trying to do?"

"Well, the little girl, evacuee, Devlin (we used to call him the 'Black Priest' then), was trying to corrupt her. But not like Josh here. It was dangerous all the same. He would follow her around and get her to do naughty things, like tie a burning twig to the cat's tail. Even had her wee in the milk churn. But the worst happened when he came one night when they was a-bombing us from the air. He tried to get her open the blackout curtains with all the lights on. He wanted the Jerries, like to blow us all to smithereens. Well Miss Cartwright weren't 'aving none of that malarkey."

"So how did she defeat him?"

"Well, she had an idea to give him so much energy so that we blasted him to the next field, afore he knew what had happened. Mavis, begging yer pardon miss, if you's think I am over familiar, calling her that, well she had us all, creatures and everything give him energy."

"Well wouldn't that make him more powerful?" I asked, puzzled.

"Yes, Miss. The blast of energy pushed 'im through the walls and into the fields beyond the back of the 'ouse, Miss. We looks out the window at 'im and he looked so powerful and intent on coming back at us."

"What happened to stop that?"

"Well, Miss, what he didn't realise until it was too late was that he was so bright with energy Miss, that the Jerries, well they bombed 'im. It don't kill a ghost none if they get bombed but he had manifested so bright and solid with alls that energy, that his atoms were blasted all over the place and I reckon it took a fair year or two afore they had all found each other agin!"

I laughed. "Ha, ha, so he can be defeated if we did something similar?"

"Sadly not, Lass. He would remember what happened before and be prepared for that one again. Besides, if my knowledge of current affairs is correct, it doesn't look like the Germans are going to bomb us any time soon. All in the past now, eh?" put in Arthur.

"And he also said that you were related, Edward?"

"Well if that is true Miss, then I can only apologise for that Miss," said Edward, ashamedly.

"That could still be useful."

"How's that, Miss?" asked Edward as Arthur stared intently.

"Well, I know very little about witchcraft. But I once had a customer, in my hairdressing salon who used to think she knew everything about it. She often told me that if you have something personal belonging to someone, like a few hairs or toenail clippings then you can make them do something. She reckoned that is how she got her fellow to love her. Oh, and she told me a horrible tale about how she wrapped some hairs, from someone she hated, around a thorn and then pierced a snail with the thorn so that it eventually died. She said that she had made that person ill for a week."

"So, that is why you took some of Patrick's hair, my girl?" remarked Arthur.

"Yes, and I was thinking that if we had something from Edward, like a cutting of his hair, then we could maybe give that to Jane. Might be that if Edward is a descendant of Devlin's then maybe, Jane would be able to tell us more about him. It is a long-shot, but maybe worth a try."

"But any hair I had has been blown in the wind, or was used to make bird nests so that some young hatchlings could keep warm. All the rest was probably buried with me, along with my bones, and me toenails too. But you is welcome to 'ave me dug up, Miss, if you's thinks it gonna help. Me grave weren't marked though as I weren't rich enough to 'ave nothing but a wooden cross. That rotted years ago. And I am under lots of brambles now in the left corner of the churchyard."

"No, we haven't gotten time to do that I don't think."

"Hang-on! I just remembered. I got a tooth, in the loft, what used to be my room. I felled off a gate and smacked me jaw. Couple of days later it popped out! Do you think that might work? That ain't rotted, I don't think. I put it in a nook in the rafters just 'oping that the fairies might come and leave me half a bob. Never, 'appened though and is 'surred it is still there."

"Yes, that might do. Worth a chance. Bring it with you tomorrow, when we go to meet Jane."

The lovers stirred from their steamy mass and Josh got up. He looked spent, but also slightly embarrassed as if he was a little ashamed as to how things had gone so far beyond his expectations.

"I think that I had better be going."

He stood up and started to dress.

Patrick said, "Oh, I thought we could do it again. I have still got one more left in me."

"I am really pleased that it helped you," Josh spoke sincerely.

"Helped me? Helped me in what way?"

"Your injury, from work. It looks your doctor was right."

Tina jabbed Patrick in the rib. "Oh, yes. My injury. You have helped to cure me young man, so you have. Did you want to stay longer and help me more?"

"Let the lad go," interjected Tina. "You run along me lad. Besides me and Patrick have a few things to discuss, haven't we Pat?"

"Have we?" asked a worried looking Patrick.

Tina sat up. "Josh, darling, give us a kiss before you go." Josh looked uncertain but bent forward. Tina gave him a passionate but loving kiss. I started to think that maybe she had started to feel some affection for him, until she asked, "Same again next week, eh lad?"

Josh nodded. "I think so," but he didn't look so certain. He then left, looking slightly dazed.

"So what do you want to discuss, Tina?" asked a concerned Patrick when they knew the Josh was out the back door.

"You very nearly screwed things up here. Luckily, I saved the day. But I enjoyed it."

"I thought it was the best sexual experience I ever had," Patrick replied. "But I am curious about one thing."

"What's that?" Tina asked.

"Well, how much compensation do you think I am due from that accident I 'ad at work?"

They both chuckled.

"And you said you still got some more in you to give me, have you?" asked Tina.

"Definitely for you my love." He rolled over a bit on the bed and started kissing her whilst pushing his fingers up into the moistness, between her legs. She moaned and pushed herself harder, onto his hand. Patrick became harder again and they started to talk out their fantasy of killing Josh. But this time it didn't seem like they thought it was a fantasy any more.

Chapter 16

Defensive tactics

The next day I went to the tree and took the hairs of Patrick with me. Edward was waiting by the old Beech and had manifested. I was still unseen to Jane, but I felt that she had sensed my presence.

"She is here, now, Miss, Jane, Jane, Miss!" he introduced us.

"I can feel her here, your friend Edward, but I can't see her," Jane told him.

"No, you won't. That's is why you have to go into the tree. Miss, will see you in there and you should see her as well. She wants to ask you to do some things, as I e'splained. I have already told the tree that you are both going in for a parley. The tree is prepared and expecting yous."

"Alright, I will try my hardest to get my whole mind in this time," she replied.

She then proceeded to place her hand on the bole of the tree, and closed her eyes deep in concentration. I did the same, standing next to her. Within a few seconds I was completely inside the tree.

Since my first time I had learnt a few things as to how to master the environment around me. I turned an area into a comfortable room. This space was devoid of all the distractions the tree could offer us, which would have detracted from my mission. It was an illusion but it would make Jane feel at ease, seeing me for the first-time. Jane was having a bit of difficulty in getting inside and I could feel her exhaustive efforts. I channelled some of my energy to her and tried to pull her in to make things easier for her. The tree also gave her a helping hand. Not long after, Jane had successfully transferred her mind into the tree. It took her a few more moments to adjust to the space I had created. When she finally adjusted and looked at me she shrieked,

"I know you, I have seen you before."

"You saw me in the house. When you were ghost-hunting with Mitch and Keith. I let out the energy, and you saw me then?"

"No, I know you. You're famous. You're the model who went missing. You are Angela Deane."

"Oh, the modelling. I had almost forgotten about that. The face-cream girl. I mainly remember my work as a hairdresser in Walsham, before I did that." I almost found it amusing that I had totally blocked that part of my life out. What else might I not remember? Jane knowing my name and this much about me. Why, why would that be? I was thinking.

"The modelling was fun but it wasn't what I had intended to do, forever. So to me, it had never seemed so important as what else I accomplished in life," I told her.

"But you were more than that. You were the face of *'Cielo amarillo''* face cream. You were in all the top magazines. You were even in an advert on the Tele. Some big talent agent had spotted you at Norwich station and offered you the job. He had been tasked with finding the new face of *'Cielo amarillo''*. Also, you had scored more goals for our local football team than any girl before. I remember when I was really little, going to a fete, and you were there, looking so beautiful and happy. You even turned on the Christmas lights one year. All the girls at school wanted to be you," Jane had excitedly jumbled this out.

I remembered then. Being approached by the agent at the train station. I had been rushing back to catch the train. He approached me and said that he wanted me for a modelling job. I initially had thought that he was just using a cheesy chat-up line. I also thought that he might want other things of me, and so leapt away from him and onto my train. He jumped on as well. Even though he had been meaning to go to go to London, and didn't have a ticket for the Norwich-to-Sheringham line. He produced a card. I read the name on the card. 'James Barnes, Modelling Agent'. And I thought that anyone could have a card made. He then took some magazines out of a case and showed me that his name was printed as the agent for some of the top-most models in the country. I recognised the famous names.

He stayed over in a North Walsham hotel that night and travelled via taxi to Suffield to meet my parents. Before long I had let my shop to a friend who was also a hairdresser. I hadn't wanted to let go of it because I knew that modelling was such a fickle world and that I would have to have a back-up plan. At the time my biggest wish would've been for my ex-boyfriend to see my picture and to fall back in love with me as we had once been. In reality, if he had ever seen my success, it would have intimidated him and driven him farther away. I would never know now what might have been.

"It is strange how I had forgotten about all of that," I lamented. "It no longer seems of any importance."

Jane looked at me still in a state of awe. "But how is it that you are here? People have been looking for you for almost 10 years. Ever, since you went missing over the Christmas period of 1984. There have been countless investigative journalists writing in the papers. Every anniversary they ask for witnesses to come forward. There have been documentaries made about you. What happened?" she, excitedly, asked me.

"Well I came to speak to you. As Edward explained," I replied puzzled.

"But how did you die? Why did you go missing? Oh, I have a thousand questions I need to ask you all at once."

"I am sorry Jane, but I can't tell you any of that. I don't fully know myself. I just know that I am meant to be here. And that is all I can tell you on that!" I remembered what Arthur had said about witches still having human flaws and I wanted to bring her back on track and not to start a wasted journey into things which didn't seem important at the moment.

Jane immediately sensed my harsher tone.

"I am sorry," she said. "I am being insensitive. Please forgive me. What do you need me to do?"

I explained to her my plan. I wanted her to find out where Patrick and his wife Vivian lived. I explained about the hairs I had taken from Patrick's head and how the trees would help her find the address where they lived. Get Viv' on her own. Maybe, go to the care home where she worked, on the day before Patrick was to come here, and tell her about the affair between Tina and Patrick. "We have to stop Patrick from turning up at the rendezvous next week."

Jane looked aghast. "That is an awful thing to do," she said. "I thought that by becoming a witch I would be using my powers for the good of people. Not to go around and condemn them, and break up their marriages."

"You may actually be saving a marriage. Plus, a young man's life is at stake. That is worth several marriage break-ups to protect him."

I then started to explain a bit about Josh – without actually saying who he was. I wanted to protect his dignity from further damage, somehow. I gave her a brief summary and mentioned the demon Devlin. She stopped me.

"Can you describe him to me please?"

I conjured up the image I had seen in the stone. Jane looked slightly frightened, so I dismissed the image.

"I know him," she told me.

"Know him?"

"Yes, Mary Gunn, the previous witch, she wrote about him in the notes she left for me."

"What did she write?" I asked thinking that power lies in knowledge.

"She wrote that his real name was 'Rodger Merriment'."

"That is his name? It sounds more like the name of a Jolly Pirate rather than an evil incarnate demon. How did she know this?"

"She knew this because he was a witch-hunter during the 1640s and through the tumult of the English Civil war. He put a lot of witches and innocents to death after torturing them for days sometimes. He got real pleasure from that torture. He was a failed clergyman who became Judge, Jury and Executioner. Villages and towns paid for him to come and cleanse their area of those they believed worshipped the devil. He was in league with Matthew Hopkins, The Witch-finder General. He also haunted Miss Gunn and she knew that he would eventually destroy her."

I felt a shudder go through Jane and knew her concern that we would be tackling this particular demon. However,

I was ecstatic knowing what Jane had just imparted. This knowledge could help us win. I went across to her and gave her a hug. Even though she wasn't fully in the tree, as I was, she felt that hug and seemed to beam with pride at my approval.

"Thank you so much for that, Jane."

"Do you still want me to tell his wife about the affair as well? I mean, with the hairs you have I could make a spell to give him diarrhoea or something. That would stop him from coming."

I stood back and looked at her. She really didn't want to tell Viv' about Patrick's affair with Tina. However, I thought, with great power comes great responsibility.

"On second thoughts," I said and paused. She looked expectantly for a reprieve. "On second thoughts, do the both. Tell his wife and give him a dose of the Trots! Believe me, he deserves it. And if one won't stop him, no harm in a back-up plan is there?"

She relaxed and we smiled in mutual respect.

When we came out of the tree, I explained to Edward some more about who Devlin was and what we planned to do. He looked slightly disappointed.

"Well, I suppose you won't be needing me tooth? I brought it 'ere all especially, like."

"No, I don't think we will. Although best ask Jane. She might know of some potion she could grind it into which might defend against our Jolly Rodger! But if there is a chance of it backfiring on you then I wouldn't want to take that chance. After all, it is your tooth and not his. Just a small amount of him in it."

Edward asked Jane if she needed his tooth and she said no. Then he brightened.

"I know, I'll bury it here. Right amongst the roots of the old lady **B**eech. It'll be the last bit of me body to be returned to the ground. And I couldn't wish for a betterer spot. Maybe, one day, it'll break down into the soil and when this 'ere old lady passes, the atoms from my tooth will help her daughter growed up big and strong. Just like her." He beamed with pleasure.

I made sure that Jane was handed Patrick's hairs via Edward. She could no longer see me now that we were outside.

She spoke to Edward, "Ask Angela if she wants me to go and let her dad know that she is OK?"

I wondered why she hadn't mentioned both of my parents. Obviously, my Mum would have passed. Maybe, just maybe, I had even been on the other side at that time to ease her crossing? I shook my head and told Edward the reasons why.

"No, Miss says, best to leave it as he would think you were some sort of crackpot."

"But I could tell him something which she told me that only the two of them would know?"

Edward gave me an enquiring look. Then he turned to Jane and said, "That's a firm, 'No'. I would nought push it no further if I was you."

Jane then left. Promising to do what I had asked of her.

When we were back at the house I insisted to Arthur and Edward that we should bring Tilly in and up-to-date, on the situation.

"Very awkward and dangerous that could be," gruffed Arthur.

"I think I know how to tell her and regain her trust," I said.

Edward also agreed that we should bring her into our circle. "She is awfully strong and she knows something is wrong with us. If we don't let her know, it could go bad for us."

Arthur reluctantly agreed. He called Tilly back in from play, for me to speak to her.

"Tilly."

"Yes Mama?" she asked with a slightly suspicious tone.

"You know what the rocks warned you about, with Josh and Tina?"

Tilly's eyes darkened over. "Yes Mama?"

"Well, Tina now wants to keep Josh to herself. She wants him to permanently stay in the house. She doesn't want him to go off and have his own family!"

Tilly suddenly leapt up. A huge amount of energy was released and her soul whizzed around the house about three times in succession. She then returned to me. She glowered at me and said, "I never liked Tina. She won't hurt Josh. I will stop her from hurting him, even if I hurt her."

"OK dear. Whatever, you feel best, my dear."

Instantly relations between the four of us eased. It was like a leaden weight had been lifted from the atmosphere in the house. We were now back to being 'a team of four'.

The next day Edward came in excitedly. He told us that he had just met with Jane and she had told him that the witches' book had suggested that there was a way that a demon could be imprisoned in a rock.

"I thought that the rock had to accept you in?" muttered a sceptical Arthur.

"Well that's the thing," Edward told us. "It was on the list of things Mistress Gunn wanted me to give to the next witch what come along. Jane, that is. The second thing I was to give her was a rock, from the box in the workshop. I'd almost forgot it. But now is the time to give it to her. When I told Jane, 'bout it she said that the rock was mentioned in Mistress Gunn's notes. It was special for catching a demon in. But it might only hold it for abouts twenty minutes to half hour. She is outside. With your permission I will invite her in to get the rock?"

We all agreed and within ten minutes Jane was standing in the parlour in front of us with the rock in one hand and the book of spells in the other.

Edward, prompted by us, asked Jane how the rock was to be used to house Devlin.

"It would help me if I could see you all," she said. "You could use the energy from the book if you need to."

Arthur said, "We can, but only for a short while. We don't want to attract the attention of this 'Roger Merriment'. I still can't get used to that name, though. Doesn't quite sound how I picture him. Still, having a demon's real-name, gives us power, which he won't expect."

We materialised and Jane, again, stood looking in awe. She loved Arthur's uniform, and thought that Tilly was adorable.

"Well, from what I have read so far, we need to place the rock in a spot close to where the demon will materialise. There is a chant I can sing, which will get the witch-finders curious about the rock. As he gets closer, then it will need all of your energies to, basically, push him in."

"Sound's simple enough," I said, "though I think that it may be dangerous for you to be so close, Jane."

"Oh, I can be in another room. The song I chant can resonate through the walls of the building. It may even amplify its effect. You will be best disposed to place the rock in the room where you feel the demon will appear. I will do the rest."

"That'll be the bedroom. We can put it there in a short-while," Edward spoke to Jane.

"Hmm, I am not so sure this will all work, my girl," muttered Arthur.

"Well if we factor out Patrick, believe that Viv' knowing will prevent his coming, and hold the demon off for 20 minutes then I doubt Tina would go ahead and…" I paused as I glanced sideways at Tilly, "hurt Josh." Tilly looked angry.

"No, I don't think that a 20-minute pause in proceedings would be enough to stop Merriment," said Arthur. "We need to get him out of here quickly, somewhere he won't be back in a hurry. And I think that, with Edward's and Jane's assistance, and the old lady Beech, I maybe have a solution."

"She won't hurt Josh, nor will he – the demon. I will stop them," stated an adamant Tilly, with menace in her voice.

Arthur told us his idea, and Edward and Jane agreed that it sounded a good one. "I'll talk to the tree tomorrow and see if it can be done safely," Edward told us.

We still had five days to go before Josh was due to meet Tina. I spent some time in following Mr. O'Connell on a couple of his walks across vast stretches of Norfolk countryside. Always ending in some out-of-the-way, church. He hadn't passed by the house recently. But as Edward had suggested, I picked up his trail by using the trees.

Edward had also returned to us the following day to let us know that the old lady Beech tree, said, "It could be done and that she was more than willing to help!"

I tried out improving the communication via the automatic-writing tool. I didn't rope Mr. O'Connell into our plans. Instead, although at first, it seemed slightly selfish, I began to get him to question what had happened to me. I felt that if anyone would convince my dad that I was OK since I passed, then it would be Mr. O'Connell. When the time was right.

In the meantime, I thought, by utilizing his journalistic skills I might get him to find some clues as to what happened to me. Also, I believed, it would help to, maybe, take his mind off his grief and help him be a better parent to Josh.

So I thought, 'Whatever, happened to Angela Deane? What was the truth behind her mysterious disappearance?' Eventually he began to write along the lines of: 'She left her friend's house on December 30th, 1984. But she never got home. Her dad was distraught. Her mother inconsolable. What if something like that happened to Josh? If the unthinkable happened and he suddenly disappeared without a trace. I can't imagine that amount of grief. The not knowing is the worse. I should look into whatever happened to her. Her father is a good man.'

The brain worm had been set free to roam his waking thoughts.

Just a few more days until Josh arrived again. Things began to get tense. Jane, knowing her tasks now, and having been let more into the secrets of what was going on, began to hone her learning towards demon fighting. She deserved a place at the table. Without her we would never have learnt who Devlin really was. She concentrated on anything she could discover about Rodger Merriment, and anything about demonology. We were all afraid that our plans would somehow be scuppered. All except Tilly.

She was the most certain amongst us. Nothing was going to happen to Josh whilst she was around.

The day before Josh was due to arrive we checked over our plans of defence. We looked for unexpected scenarios. Arthur had set up an operation room in the loft. Tilly and Josh had managed to sketch a few things out and Arthur had pinned these against the plaster of a supporting wall. He placed bits of string between the keywords and pictures. He carried out numerous briefings. He had taken to wielding a stick to point out courses of actions, causes and effects. He ended each briefing with the same words each time, "Remember, the word 'Ops' stands for 'Opportunities' as well as 'Operations'. Think on your feet. If during the action you see an opportunity, change tack and take another path. Never let the enemy second-guess you. We are strong because of our ability to adapt." He was our leader, and we loved him.

This afternoon I gave Jane a last briefing. It was her job to scupper the Patrick element. She seemed more confident and set off from the Beech tree fully understanding her responsibility.

Much later that evening, she recounted to us what had happened.

"Well, I found out from the tree where Patrick and Viv lived. From there it was easy to find details of where Viv worked. She had a shift this evening at the Grange care-home in Horsted. I went there just before she ended her shift and told someone on reception that I urgently needed to talk to her. She came to reception and I asked her if we could talk outside. Which we did. She was very curious to know why I had turned up there. It was at this point that I became very nervous and wished that I was anywhere else on the planet than here. Believe, me when I say, that she is a lovely lady, with a radiant spirit. Vivian never deserved to be caught up in this. And I began to hate Patrick even more, though I didn't know him at all.

"I told her about the affair and that they had been using a disused house for their liaisons. That I had seen them there whilst out for a walk. At first she thought that I was a trouble-maker and wouldn't believe me. She told me to leave her in peace and that this was some sort of sick joke. Then I did as you mentioned, Angela. I described the tattoo on his buttocks. She started to cry. I mentioned Tina's name and she instantly knew that what I said was true. She said that she had rather never known. I told her that she had to stop Patrick from meeting Tina the next day. Viv left work slightly earlier than she should have and went straight home."

"So that was the end of it?" I asked.

"Not exactly," She said. "I think that one of the other staff had seen us talk. They must have seen me walk down the road, and across into the 'Sargeant' pub. I needed a stiff drink or two to steady my nerves. I felt awful about what I had just done, even though I knew it to be the right thing to do. Then things got a little unpredictable."

"What happened?" asked a concerned Edward. I think he felt that he should have been on-hand to protect Jane.

"Well, I had been in the pub for about half an hour, and was about to leave and come back to you all, when the door burst open. In walked a livid Patrick. Someone must have told him who and where I was. He looked around and his eyes settled on me, sitting alone as I was to one side. He marched over and started shouting, calling me a ' bitch and a wicked witch'. He was so angry that I got really scared. I could tell that others in the bar were trying to ignore us because they thought it just a domestic argument and that they didn't want to get involved. I felt really vulnerable, and got more frightened the closer he got.

"Well, he started hollering and shouting at me. Said that I had been seen at the care home and that I was just some useless slut and an interfering witch. He made like he was going to drag me out to the car park and beat me."

Edward looked very angry and concerned all at once. "The soulless fiend. Whatever 'appened?" he asked.

Well I suddenly felt brave. I thought what would Angela do? I stood my ground and told him that he was correct, that I was a witch, but not as wicked as he was. Then I spoke out loud the spell I had prepared, and he just stood there dumbfounded. Then it worked, I was so pleased. My first real spell.

"Wot worked?" Edward asked.

"Well, he shat himself. Right in the middle of the saloon bar. At first you heard a gurgling sound, just like he was really hungry. He looked down and suddenly there was a nauseating smell which engulfed the pub. And Patrick's jeans turned brown. He couldn't believe what had just happened. He barely hobbled to the loo when the next lot burst out over his belt and through the bottom of his trousers. He left a trail of liquid squit across the carpet. I wouldn't be surprised if he wasn't still there, in the loo, trying to clean himself up. Cleared the pub of customers. The smell was awful. By my reckoning he should lose a couple of pounds in weight over the next few days and be out-of-action for a while!"

"Well, that sounds like he has been dealt with well and truly. Now we just have to concentrate on the other two," said a relieved Arthur. "Best you get yourself home now, Lass, it is already late. You'll need all the sleep you can get. Edward you could walk her home maybe?"

"That's OK. I can kip here tonight. Save going all the way back and forth. After all, it isn't as if I am going to get haunted or anything, is it?" replied Jane.

She slept in my blue room that night on a clean sheet we found in a closet. It was good to have the company. Strange really. If somebody had told me a few weeks previously that I would have powered-down in a room with a living person in, I probably would have run a mile.

Chapter 17

The fight and the storm

When the day arrived, we were all on edge. Jane had arrived previously and set up in the basement. The more I had gotten to know her the more that I liked her. She hadn't gone to a secondary school like me but to Norwich school for girls, followed by a private school in Holt.

Like me, she was also sporty. My drug was football. Hers was hockey. She had been Captain of her team. But what impressed me most about her was that she didn't seem like someone from the 'Horsey-set'. You would normally imagine that someone from such an elite background would be a bit 'stuck-up', but she had remained more down-to-earth.

"When you get the rock, run like hell!" I told her.

"No need to tell me that, I will be there in a blink of an eye!" She smiled at me.

I recited, "Faster than a speeding bullet. More powerful than a locomotive. Able to leap tall buildings in a single bound. Look! Up in the sky! It's a bird! It's a plane! It's SuperJane! Yes, it's SuperJane!" Jane had joined me at mid-pointy in this superhero mantra. And at the end we both fell about laughing. I materialised enough for us both to hug for a few moments.

"Look, whatever you do, stay safe. OK?" I finally requested. "If things seem to get out of hand then get the hell out."

She nodded back at me.

"Did you call the security firm in Norwich?"

"Yes, Ang, just as you asked. Called him from a phone box. I managed to speak to Suhaib and told him that some kids had decided to use drugs in the house today, before noon and that they were talking about burning the place down. I said that he should get some back-up from the local fuzz. When he asked my name, I just hung up. Seems my main destiny as a witch is to tell tales on people. I believe that he took it seriously!" Jane reassured me.

Tina arrived and looked around for Patrick. He was nowhere in sight. She called his name.

Tilly remained behind the screen in the bedroom. Her mood was darker than black. She fumed. She was stealthily building energy like a leopard ready for the pounce of death.

"Useless, prick, so he is!" Tina said out loud.

Then she spoke aloud again, but to herself this time. "If he ain't here, and Josh don't turn up, then I am out-ta-here. I ain't 'aving some deranged kid staring at me in the mirror again!"

She moved nervously around the place until she heard some other sounds.

Josh arrived.

"Damn," I said to Arthur, "I thought that he would have been too embarrassed by the last encounter to show up again. At least, that is what I was hoping for."

"No," spoke Arthur, "it is in our human nature to seek out our own destruction. Unfortunately, it seems to be the way of the world. We tend to think that what we are offered in life is part of our destiny and always needs to be consumed. Then we follow that path, and our destiny often turns and leads us down a dark road.

"He is a young man. Like a blinkered horse, he follows the route of least resistance. Sees himself as some kind of bohemian 'artist'. For his ego to have credibility he must seek out the dangerous path. It is unfortunate, but it is in his nature. It takes a lot of moral courage to stand back and look at your options, and seek the wisest ones. Decide to leave some paths to one side and to take the toughest route. And, even then, mistakes can still be made."

"Hello darling, have you seen Patrick about outside? He was meant to meet me down the lane, but his car wasn't where he normally parks. I thought he may have parked a bit nearer but I can't see him nowhere around."

Josh answered, "No, I walked through the woods. I didn't see anybody that way."

"Oh well, he's probably just running late. We can be getting on whilst we wait, can't we?" Tina seemed less confident than I had seen her before.

I had been right. Without Patrick around, I was sure, nothing was going to happen to Josh. We had saved the day. All we needed now, was for Suhaib to turn up and turf them out. They were trespassing. We had probably put an end to the whole diabolical episode.

Tilly appeared. She had sensed Josh's arrival. She glared at Tina. I put out a hand to steady her from doing anything. "It is alright, Tilly. Mama thinks that Tina is going to let Josh go." Tilly stayed by my side. But still seemed highly suspicious of Tina.

Tina moved over to Josh. She kissed him gently and slowly in what seemed like an almost loving gesture. Definitely nothing bad was going to happen today. I spoke to Tilly and told her that Tina was just going to kiss and cuddle Josh, because he missed his mum. That I was sure that this was going to be the last time. That Tina would then let Josh get on with his life. And that it was alright for her to go and play by the bank if she had enough energy.

Tilly was reassured. Even she could tell that Tina was being gentle. Tilly left.

After a while of tender passions there arose a more erotic fever between the two. The inevitable happened. Tina took Josh's hand and led him to the bedroom upstairs.

"Well, that's it then," I said to Arthur. "I think that we can leave them alone to get on with things and I would imagine, Josh'll move on with the whole experience in his back pocket."

Arthur looked doubtful, "Things are never as straight forward as that." I heard a distant roll of thunder. The sky darkened outside and rain began to fall.

"Looks like we're going to have a thunderstorm, after all of the glorious sunshine we've been having lately," I reflected.

Arthur still looked concerned. "That's a bad omen. If we get lightning too then the energy released can be a stimulant for demons. Encourages them out of their holes and from beneath their rocks."

Lightning suddenly flashed and lit up the darkened sky. I felt the trees outside tremble, as if they were frightened. This heightened sense scared me. I felt complete vulnerability, all of a sudden.

I wondered if it was just my imagination working over-time, and if Arthur was being slightly melodramatic. Then we were taken by surprise.

We heard the scream upstairs.

We both looked worriedly at each other and appeared in the bedroom upstairs to see what was going on. Edward came up from the cellar where he had been keeping Jane company.

"What's going on?" he asked. Then everything seemed to happen at once.

Josh was slapping Tina. She was begging him to strike her, laughing manically. Josh's eyes were red. Devlin was inside him. Rodger Merriment possessed him.

Something scuttled in the room beside me. I looked down and to my left. Stalking me like a hyena was a strange looking creature which had the face of a gargoyle, the wings of a pigeon and was walking on extended, Cockerel-like claws.

"What is that?" I shrieked.

"It is a sleep daemon!" cried Arthur, "Merriment has brought along an accomplice."

The thing snarled at me. It was the most horrible creature imaginable. Evil seeped from it like negative energy. Dark, black, sickly energy. I felt a wave of nausea come over me. If ghosts could be physically sick I would have vomited right at that moment.

"We haven't got two rocks. What are we going to do? We didn't plan for two demons."

Arthur took firm control, "Keep it together, Lass. Edward, go to Jane and tell her to begin the incantation for the spell. Use your energy to fend that thing off. Remember what I taught you, Angela. Think of the bigger picture. Sleep Daemons are cowardly by nature. That is why they seldom attack somebody sleeping in a house with pets."

I did as Arthur suggested. I used all my effort. Arthur addressed the main demon, Merriment. Merriment had gone into Tina. She was thrusting herself harder each time onto Josh's groin. Her head turned towards me and the sleep daemon. The thing didn't seem put out by my energy. It looked like it was going to pounce on me at any moment.

Tina addressed the daemon. It looked away from me towards her. "Fetch!" she told it, her eyes a horrific, dark red.

The daemon turned around and went out of the door and I heard it scuttle down the stairs.

'Where had it gone?' I wondered. I became fearful for the safety of Edward and Jane, lest it ambush them in the cellar.

I needn't have worried, it returned a few moments later. It had gotten a knife from the kitchen. It went over to Tina, as it did so, Arthur saw the danger and called, "Tilly, you're needed."

Too late the knife had been handed over to Tina who returned her focus on Josh.

Tilly appeared. She saw the sleep daemon, then she vanished again.

I thought out loud. "It frightened her! That thing scared Tilly."

"I don't think so my dear," said Arthur. "It would take more than a sleep daemon to scare Tilly."

Tilly returned to the room. She had something large and brown with her. It was the house rat. The house rat saw the sleep daemon. It hissed and seemed to grow to twice its size. The sleep daemon seemed petrified. It turned and ran out of the door quickly followed by the rat.

Tina stabbed at Josh. The first slash, cut his arm. Josh yelped and jumped backwards. Tilly unleashed a huge amount of energy at Tina. She hesitated on her second stab and Josh moved quickly towards the wardrobe. Arthur made the doors slam shut before he had a chance to get in. I looked at him.

"Sorry, Lass, but if I let him climb in there then he will be a sitting target." He shrugged his shoulders. Josh ran into the upstairs hallway and made his way downstairs. Blood from his cut arm had smeared across the doors of the wardrobe where he had run into them as they closed. A trail of blood followed his path. He was bleeding quite a lot.

Tina jumped up and went to follow him out. She still lusted for his death. Edward materialised in time to see Tilly manifest in front of Tina, blocking her exit. She had the most severe expression on her face. Suddenly Tilly hissed and leapt at Tina. Tina jumped backwards and toppled the screen. It tipped over. As it did so it revealed Jane's rock. Suddenly, the room was filled with Jane's incantation.

"That's what I came up to tell yous. Jane said that it will start to work about now," Edward informed us. It had. Rodger Merriment looked stunned as he appeared outside of Tina. He was staring in baffled astonishment at the rock on the floor.

Tilly leapt at Tina, who lay on her back on the floor. Tina screamed and slashed at her with the knife. The knife went harmlessly through Tilly. Tina stabbed herself by mistake a couple of times in the legs. She screamed hysterically.

"Get off of me, you devil child."

Tilly, leapt at her again and again. Then, she presented herself as a half-decomposed cadaver. Grey, with maggots crawling out of her eye sockets and she bared her soil covered teeth and hissed. Her face up close to Tina's face. Tina screamed, covered her eyes and started to cry.

Tilly stood back. Became her pretty self again. She put her hands on her hips and turned towards Merriment.

"Rodger Merriment, are you leaving us?" asked Edward.

Merriment turned, astonished.

"Where did you learn my name you whelp?" he rasped the question, "been doing your family tree, have ye?"

"Never mind that," Edward said.

Merriment looked back at the rock. It almost throbbed from Jane's incantation. He moved closer to it. Then he turned as if he was going to take us all on. We stood together, looking at him. Then Edward asked him,

"What comes first, the chicken or the egg?"

Merriment looked back at him as if he had gone mad.

"What?"

"I said ol' fellow, 'What comes first? The chicken or the egg?' "

"The chicken or the egg?"

"Simple question," said Edward. He repeated, "What comes first the chicken or the egg?"

Edward kept repeating it.

Merriment was astonished as if Edward were trying to ask a riddle. He started to repeat, as if he didn't understand Edward's logic and questioned his sanity.

Then we used our energy and pushed him into the rock.

He went in and before he knew he was there, he had asked the rock, "What comes first, the chicken or the egg?"

We weren't privy to the rock's answer but felt sure that Edward, with his quick thinking had got him more than 20 minutes of jail time.

"Edward, could you please ask Jane to join us?"

Tilly turned around. "Best be quick, Suhaib is driving down the track."

Jane came into the room a few minutes later.

The storm was still raging outside.

She quickly took up the rock and put it in a small backpack and slung her arms through the straps. She grinned at me as we had all materialised to give her help and encouragement.

"You have to be careful. Suhaib and his deputy will be here in a moment. Also, it is chucking it down outside. I don't like the thought of you going out when there is lightning about. Especially in a wood, with all the trees. It's not safe."

"I'll be fine," she reassured me, "hockey champion – remember!"

"Well, this footballer, and Arthur, will meet you by the Beech tree when you arrive. Edward will keep at your heels and inform us if you get into any difficulties. Tilly's just gone to find Josh. She says he is in one of the outbuildings sheltering from the storm. So avoid Josh and Suhaib, if you can. It wouldn't be good to be seen."

"See you shortly," she said, and she shot off out of the door and down the stairs.

We watched her from the window as she quickly ran past the back of the out buildings and through the bush which hid the gap in the fence. She was running like the wind and into the woods before the security car pulled up. It had flashing orange lights on top. A few minutes later Suhaib had unlocked the gates of the perimeter fence and driven it through, on to the paved area. He had two people with him. As he got out of the vehicle Josh came out of the workshop and approached Suhaib, whilst holding the injured arm. Tilly stood behind him.

"What's going on?" asked Suhaib.

"There's a crazy lady – in there – with a knife. She stabbed me." Josh indicated the house.

Suhaib took a look at Josh's arm and indicated to one of his deputies to get the first aid kit from the truck.

The other deputy headed towards the back door of the house. "Where do you think you're going?" Suhaib asked the man.

"To get the crazy lady," he replied.

"Not on my watch, you're not. I am not having one of our members of staff stabbed. We leave that bit to the proper authorities."

Suhaib then got on his walkie-talkie and called the security firm to send the police he had spoken to earlier. He told them about the knife attack and that they might need an ambulance for a lad who had been stabbed in his left, upper. Arm."

I heard sobbing and looked around. Tina had squeezed herself into the corner of the room behind the bed. She was bleeding from her legs quite a bit.

Compassionately, I asked, "Shouldn't we get her some help?"

Arthur gruffed, "I am back in the 'not meddling mode', my dear! Besides, you just heard Suhaib, the police are on their way. Shouldn't take them long to get here from Hoveton.

He was right. They were there within 15 minutes, and in the bedroom in a further two minutes. A couple of large officers with truncheons to the ready. They soon found the sobbing Tina, who kept going on about a demonic child who had attacked her. The two coppers glanced at each other and shook their heads. You could see that they were thinking she was completely mad. One of them used a handkerchief to pick the knife up. He wrapped it and stowed it for evidence. The other tore a sheet and bandaged her legs. We heard the ambulance arrive.

Arthur said, "Right – Jane should be at the tree about now. We should go. Everything is taken care of here."

We materialised at the tree as Jane came slipping and sliding, through the mud, along the last bit of path. She deftly skipped over other gnarled tree roots on the way. Rain water was cascading down her face and she looked soaked through. But she looked ever so pleased with herself and the speed at which she had gotten here.

I warned her, "The tree is slippery with all the rain. It is going to be difficult to climb to the fork in the branches we spoke about."

"Trouble with Beech trees, they is slippery at the best of times. Worse with rain."

"Who said anything about climbing?"

"How are you going to get it up there then?"

"Hate to brag, but I was also girls' school cricket champion. Played County, and almost played for England once, but got an injury. I am going to bowl it up there."

With that she took off the backpack and took out the rock.

"That's the hole you want it in, Edward? Right where the tree forks, where a branch has come away?"

"That's the one," he assured her.

"Stand back then, here goes."

With that she took a few steps back, gave a little run up and over-armed bowled the rock into the gap between the two thick branches. It hit just above and for a second looked like it was going to fall back. At the last moment it dropped neatly into the hole. I looked suspiciously down at Tilly and she gave me a secret wink.

Jane looked surprised and said, "Better than I thought. I was expecting to have two or three goes at it!

Then disaster happened. The tree was struck by lightning. The energy knocked us all backwards, but Jane went flying back more than the rest of us. Edward went to her side where she had landed on some brambles. She was still alive. We could all sense her life-force. Edward looked up, something creaked loudly. We followed his gaze upwards. One of the trees branches was splitting. Flames burning the blackened topmost end.

"Quick," shouted Edward, in panic. "Help me move her, now."

We all immediately went by them both and by using most of our energy managed to levitate Jane away from where the branch came crashing down through the foliage to where she had been, just seconds before.

We all felt tired. The energy was sapping from us. If we didn't get back to the house shortly then we would have to spend the night in the woods.

Edward leaned over Jane and unslung her backpack from her shoulder. She was semi-conscious.

"We'll have to get her back to the house so's she can recover," he told us.

"I know that is what we must do. But we haven't the energy left to carry her all the way back there," I said feeling lost.

"All of you, draw on the energy from the bag," Edward instructed us.

We did as we were asked.

Of course. The book of spells was in the backpack. It had almost boundless energy. Within seconds, we had re-charged.

"What about the tree? It is injured. Will she still be able to do what we wanted her to, Edward?" asked a concerned Arthur.

"Hang on. I am just gonna pop up and see if the rock is in the hole. If not, we'll have to levitate it back in there. Keep an eye on Jane for a moment will thee?" Within an instant, Edward was standing between the branches.

"Yup, he's still in there. I'll just check the tree is alright," he called down to us.

He then turned and entered the tree. A couple of seconds later he was back with us. "She is fine. Nothing but a few scratches. She said, 'Call that lightning? You should have been here in1967. That was a proper storm. This was just a jumped-up flash-in-the-pan.' How's Jane, now?"

"She is better now. Tilly put Jane's hand on the book of spells. It seems that ghosts aren't the only ones who can draw energy from it," said Arthur.

Just then we heard a noise above us. We looked up and we saw Rodger Merriment, aka Devlin, staring down at us. He had emerged from the rock. It had been 40 minutes. I wanted to ask him, 'Chicken or Egg?' but I never had the opportunity. He crouched down, pointed his bony finger at us. He rasped that he hadn't quite finished with us yet. Started making threats. Then he touched the side of the tree and was gone.

"I'd better check it worked," said Edward and a few seconds later he was in the tree.

He shortly returned and said, "Yup, it worked."

"So what happened to him then?" asked Arthur.

"Well the tree, it kinda whipped 'im away. It took 'im to a place called Timbuktu and deposited 'im outta another tree in the middle of nowhere. Desert all around. Just a solitary tree by a shrine. The tree then closed off all vegetation to him. He can never enter them again to have safe passage anywheres. If he wants to come back then he most likely will have to walk, and he won't know which direction," stated a very, satisfied Edward.

"Well-done, my Lad. After tonight you deserve the George Medal. You all do, in fact, "and he smiled down at Tilly especially.

We managed to get Jane back to the house. When we returned the Police and the ambulance had left. Josh was gone, and so was Tina. Suhaib and his deputies were repairing the hole in the fence. Josh must've shown them where he had gotten in. It was dark now.

We overheard some of their conversation.

"Said they were gonna take her to the nuthouse they were. Stark raving mad, she was," one of the men said to the others.

Whilst they were occupied we lifted Jane over the fence and back into the house. She slept deeply on my bed in the blue bedroom. I lay and cuddled her throughout the night. She healed.

⊷⊷⊷◀❖▶⊷⊷⊷

Chapter 18

The Conclusion

I came down the next morning and the sun was shining. It was glorious after the dark storm of the day before. Arthur was standing, lost in thought with his hands behind his back. He was staring out across the back garden.

"How are you Arthur?" I asked, "Glorious day, isn't it?"

He was back in his old clothes. Though I had already known this as I had smelt pipe tobacco on the way down.

"How is Jane?" he sullenly asked.

"Fine," I replied, "regaining her strength. She'll probably sleep until the afternoon."

"I am sorry!" he said, as if making an apology.

"Sorry? Sorry for what? We won, didn't we? You know, good championing over evil and all that? Can't see what you have to be sorry about."

He didn't answer. I began to feel worried. A cloud blocked out the rays from the morning sun and the room darkened.

"How's Edward?" I asked in a sudden panic as if something bad might have happened to him.

"Oh, Edward? He's fine. He will be back shortly. He just wanted to be by himself for a while.

"And Tilly? Is she fine too?"

"She's gone," he answered mournfully.

"What, gone, gone down by the brook to play?"

"No," he said with a sense of despair, "she is gone! I am sorry, Lass."

"Gone? Gone where?" I asked. I was confused, Arthur seemed to be talking in riddles.

"She has passed over," he said.

I was stunned.

"I don't understand," I said, not being able to comprehend the enormity of what I was being told. "She has been here longer than any of us," I said. "She has more right to be here than anybody. She loves playing by the brook. She is the strongest of us all. How can she be gone?"

"I believe that her mission was accomplished. She was probably here for Josh. Now that he has been saved from the evils of Rodger Merriment and his merry psychos, she has done what she came here to do. She has passed on. To be born again, possibly."

"I want her back," I said. I was being totally illogical, unreasonable even, and I knew it.

"I want my baby girl back." My heart was breaking. "This house needs her laughter, DON'T THEY UNDERSTAND THAT?" I shouted this last bit as if it would make the heavens relent and send Tilly back to us.

"Still hurts, doesn't it, Lass? When someone passes on. Even the dead feel that pain. Even us, those who should be the wisest and know. 'It is, because, it is'!"

We were both silent for a while.

"And Edward knows this, does he?"

"Yes Lass, he knows. That is why he has gone to spend some time alone." After a few minutes he said, "There were the others, you know?"

"Others? Like the ones, Edward mentioned, at the time of the evacuees?" I asked, picturing more Tilly's and other ghosts.

"Yes, others. Other spirits, who have come and gone. Edward, Tilly, and I, have seen a fair few and been through many adventures with them. They all passed on. When their missions were done, they all went. Same as the living, really. Once your path has been trodden, then it is time to leave. You can't hang on forever. What good would that do?"

"But I never said goodbye. And we were meant to go shopping together!" I whined. "I didn't get a chance to say goodbye. I should've been able to hold her, tell her how I loved her. Spent some time with her. I could have told her how much I have come to love her."

"Dunnia worry about that, Lass. She knew. She knew you loved her. There is one thing that stands out a mile with you, Angela, and that is how much you love those around you."

If ghosts could cry, I cried. I sobbed and sobbed.

"I hope she has a wonderful new life," I sobbed, "with the best parents ever. A couple, who love her so dearly."

"Aye, Lass, that is all we can hope for. But what will be, will be. Besides, she may spend years in the middle before she is reborn again. She might be helping others cross over."

"In the middle?"

"Heaven, the light at the end of the tunnel. You, yourself spent a while there. Years passed from you leaving here to returning."

"Once, I thought that I had only been there seconds," I reflected.

"No, you were there a while, probably helping others – as is your nature to do. You just don't remember it. I think Edward will leave here, soon, too," he said.

I was shaken further. "Why?"

"Because, and I may be wrong on this, but because I think that his mission is to guide Jane into the ways of witchcraft. Once he has done that, then he too will be gone."

"But you said that could be 2 or 3 years yet?"

"That is not a long time, my dear."

I knew that what Arthur spoke was correct.

"But we'll be alone."

"You can't hold onto fledglings forever, my dear. All birds spread their wings at some point. It is their destiny. You can't hold back time, Lass."

Again, I knew that Arthur was correct.

"What about you, Arthur? When will you go and leave me here alone?"

"Of that, my girl, I am not too sure. I still don't know my mission. Maybe it was just to be here for you. And when, you know, your mission is complete, then maybe we will fly the coop together, eh Lass?"

"But I still don't know my mission yet, Arthur. I still don't know how I passed either. So many 'Why' questions left unanswered." I told Arthur. As I did this, I thought of John O'Connell and wondered if he would provide me with the answers.

"All in good time, my dear, all in good time!"